My Intended

My Intended

A LOVE STORY

Brandi
Scollins-Mantha

EAGLE BROOK

WILLIAM MORROW AND COMPANY, INC.

NEW YORK

Published by Eagle Brook
An Imprint of William Morrow and Company, Inc.
1350 Avenue of the Americas, New York, N.Y. 10019

It is the policy of William Morrow and Company, Inc., and its imprints
and affiliates, recognizing the importance of preserving what has been
written, to print the books we publish on acid-free paper, and we exert
our best efforts to that end.

Library of Congress Cataloging-in-Publication Data

Scollins-Mantha, Brandi.
My intended : a love story / Brandi Scollins-Mantha.—1st ed.
p.   cm.
ISBN 0-688-17404-3
I. Title.
PS3569.C5846M95   2000
813'.54—dc21   99–36973
CIP

Printed in the United States of America

First Edition

1   2   3   4   5   6   7   8   9   10

BOOK DESIGN BY BERNARD KLEIN

www.williammorrow.com

To Mahesh, for helping me find the courage to commit this project and this life

Acknowledgments

Thanks to my mom, Hope, for letting me stay at the table and listen to the stories of the "tall" people. And thanks to Avram and Jen for helping me keep that tradition alive.

My Intended

Thursday, October 2, 1997

He greets me as I walk in the door. Eyes wild like a four-year-old's after a Hershey bar, tongue protruding teasingly out of his mouth, thumbs in ears, fingers splayed like moose antlers. You can almost hear a faint "nah, na, nah, na, nah, I got home first," but that would only be my imagination; in most houses, framed pictures never talk.

The first time I saw him being silly was our second meeting after returning from New Mexico. A swell of public transportationites carried me along with them up the stairs of the Ninth Street Path Station and left me stranded at the top. Looking around to orient myself, I found him standing only a few feet ahead of me on the sidewalk, his feet turned at forty-fives like a ballerina about to plié. His head was tucked to his chin, and his eyes were fixed on the space in between his feet. I nixed the thought of calling out his name; I wanted to see what he was doing first. After one meeting, you can never be sure about a person.

I stepped closer, not letting my bag fall from my shoulder and disturb him. A pigeon stood in front of him; its bird feet also about to plié. It pecked at the ground; its oily neck shimmered a rainbow of colors like a puddle of antifreeze. When the pigeon moved forward, so did Drew. He was one with the pigeon. He followed the pigeon's small footsteps for a couple of sidewalk squares, never advancing too quickly as to scare the small bird in front of him. I liked him then, all of him. The way his thighs bulged through his bicycle shorts, and how his gaze was so intent on his small, winged companion.

The bird quickened its pace, hopped, and flew away. I half expected Drew to follow. In that moment, I realized he could fly; maybe not with a pigeon, but with whatever I had to give him.

He watched his companion sail to the one tree still left on the street before turning to face me. He crossed his eyes and flapped his arms at his sides, before taking two giant steps toward me. He pressed his warm lips to my cheeks, which were red from embarrassment—not because he was acting like a recently released mental patient on the street—but because I met the one person who could read my mind without trying.

I pull the picture frame from the foyer wall and carry it down the hall to what until yesterday used to be our room. Carefully, I raise the metal tabs that hold the frame and its contents in place. I slip the picture out from under the glass and place it in my night table with the hundred other pictures of him I keep there. Pressing the metal tabs back into place, I stab my thumb. Bleed a little. Finger in mouth, like a child, I return the empty frame to the wall.

Sunday, October 19, 1997

Our apartment is not conducive to sleeping late. It is the apartment of a stockbroker in a city of stockbrokers with a built-in daylight warning system. If you are not up by eight-thirty, the sun will warm you, scald you, in fact, up and out of the bed, which becomes immersed in its sometimes glorious rays. I stumble up out into the kitchen, pulling down my favorite larger-than-necessary coffee mug from the cabinet above the sink. I pick up the once gleaming Farberware coffeepot that my best friend, Rena, sent us as an apartment-warming present. She said we would need coffee to get along in the morning. But she was wrong; we always got along fine with or without the caffeine. I realize, though, that it probably has more to do with the fact that Drew is up and out of the house before the sun can even creep into the city let alone our bedroom.

I hold the pot over my cup a few seconds before setting it down and bringing the cup up under my nose for a whiff of that good-morning smell only Kenya AA can offer. But the cup is empty; Drew didn't make coffee this morning. Nor will he any other morning, and it scares me how easily I can slip, even after just a month, into not knowing the simple fact that Drew is gone.

I look up at the calendar on the wall, the calendar I made with pictures of meadow flowers and serene, goose-covered lakes for New Jersey Manufacturers' Life Insurance. Drew hung the calendar to the right of the window to remind us, he said, of our future in the country with three kids and four big dogs. I stare at the lines through the days, feeling each one acutely, as you would feel a wound when picking off the layers of a scab. The lines lead away from the day he died and forward to our wedding day.

Wedding day, I think, removing the stick that keeps the window open. I stand a little too close as its loose frame slams into the sill. The calendar flutters up in the wake of the window. The paint on the sill is cracked and dusty from the shock of one too many abrupt blows. The glass shakes, coming apart from the wood. I press my face against its coolness and finger the fog that forms as I search the faces of the people on the street below.

My Intended

Among the joggers, the late-night party people just stumbling home, the men with strollers, the newspaper vendors, and the people frantically stocking the fruit and vegetable stands, I look for Drew or some sign of him: a hand through wavy brown hair, a silver flash of a Cannondale, a wave of a twenty-dollar bill to attract a cab, or even a small glint of sunlight off his capped left incisor. I look for him and have looked for him every day since he didn't get off that plane from Chicago. From the moment the stewardess shut the door to the ramp to the empty airplane, I've been searching the faces of strangers, trying to find him, not even to bring him back, but to get a chance to say a proper good-bye.

I foolishly thought the funeral would be my chance. I stared at the lifeless body that was once his, now puffy, hands marked black and blue from the intravenous that pumped the fluids that failed to keep him afloat. That day, I imagined his chest much the same way, singed and scarred from their attempts to make his heart stop arresting. The body was there, and I knew it was supposed to be him, but it wasn't. The lips pressed together into a waxy closemouthed smirk didn't even come close to the real way he smiled. His blue eyes shut under puffy lids covered with too much pancake makeup revealed nothing about the life that used to exist there.

And after leaving the place where I thought I was supposed to say good-bye, my search grew much larger and longer than anyone would have expected from a woman who dragged her feet about marrying him. And what makes that idea harder, prolongs it in fact, is that sometimes when I am alone or not thinking about anything at all, I can feel him. It's the same sensation you get when someone is looking at you when you're reading on the train or standing in a crowd of people. You can be reading, head down, focused on the article in front of you, and then suddenly need to look up because you feel someone watching you. I feel that a lot now and know somehow that it is Drew watching me, but when I turn around or look up, it is only the calendar on the wall or the television turned off or what used to be his favorite chair empty.

I look back at the calendar. October's scene is a field with pumpkins at dusk. Drew was with me that day, bounding around the field, holding up pumpkin after pumpkin in front of his face, trying to find one the same size as his head. *How's this?* he had asked, his voice warbled through the pumpkin, do we have a match? And then he lowered the pumpkin and smiled at me, not a jack-o'-lantern's smile, but a welcoming smile that pulled me in and made me reluctant to ever let go. I move my fingers from pumpkin to pumpkin and then down into the days of the month. I count the nineteen days of this month that I have spent without him and count the six coming days that would have made me his wife.

I dreaded those days for months, dragging my feet about wedding gowns and justices of the peace, and not because I didn't want to marry him but because I didn't want to lose Drew and our life together for a champagne-punch toast and fifty-seven yards of white satin and tulle. I just wanted it to be us—the way we were.

Now all that's left is the emptied apartment: the kitchen chair he used to hang his tie on before dinner; his coffee cup, still waiting for the first cup of the day, on the shelf next to the empty space left by mine; his shoes, now dusty and unpolished, to the left of the front door. The joke is on me, I think. Everything that I thought I was protecting left me soundlessly and a thousand miles away. And I'm not the only one who thinks it is a joke. The people who sobbed on their padded seats at the funeral home, snickered as I walked by, snickered at the woman who didn't want to marry the man who died.

What I feared most has become irrevocably true. And what hurts worst of all is that if Drew is still with me, watching me from behind a raised newspaper or floating above what used to be our bed while I sleep, he could have heard them laughing and what they were laughing about. I slide my finger back and forth over those six small days that should have led to the first and happiest of our life together. I stop on the last day, move my fingers over the curls and swoops of his handwriting. Wedding. And then over the three red lines underneath and the little heart, lopsided and scribbled underneath the lines. I trace over the *W* and *E* and the *D* and pause on the thought that I still could marry him.

I savor that thought, letting it roll and boil in my mind like a good pot of chicken soup. And just the thought of it, the thought of standing up and admitting how much I wanted to marry that man, makes me feel better than I had in weeks.

I stand on the platform in the underground train station, half enjoying the warm rush of air that precipitates the train. *Train,* I think. Would my wedding dress have a train? Have. Have had. Could still have. And I like the sound of that. *Could still have* offers some hope where I thought it couldn't ever be. It would be my way to say good-bye to the life I loved—not some chemical-filled shell that looked like someone I used to know. And I could tell everyone how I feel, and he would be there, not in a tuxedo with a white rose on his lapel, but there—watching.

The train that will take me to Ruby's house finally pulls in. I hesitate for a minute, unsure if this is the path I really want to take. Things with my mother haven't always gone the way I planned. While she is and takes pride in being my mother, too many other things add up in her life and subtract from our life together. Not that it even felt like we had a life together.

After my father died, it was more like I was always visiting, paying a social call, even though we lived in the same house. From the time I was eight years old, there was always some man around, some husband or someone trying to be a husband. I would come down to breakfast, and he'd be there. Whoever he was. I'd politely smile, watch Ruby and the man sip coffee and share the sports section of the newspaper, and then stay out of the house until I absolutely had to come back. I couldn't bear to watch her wrapped up in conversation with some guy who might or might not go the distance. I always wanted to scream at her, wave a flag around, and remind her that I never left. And I felt that very way until the day I left for college.

The train lurches quickly backwards, then forward. I grab on to the top of the nearest vinyl seat, settling into its orange folds defeatedly and next to an older woman sleeping with her head on the window. The absolute white spirals and swirls of her hair stick against the glass like icing on a cake. *A cake,* I think; *should we have a cake?* The tiers of an imaginary cake reach up in my mind hopefully. Whipped cream and butter cream and blue rosettes. Powdered sugar and strawberry filling. Or maybe bittersweet chocolate with curls of chocolate cascading like waterfalls over the tiers. But the same people who sobbed in the padded seats at the funeral home might think a cake in poor taste and find ever new things to snicker about.

My stomach shifts back and forth with the train, past the small, grungy factory cities without plant life and the metallic, austere, power-generating stations that dot the landscape on either side of the train. The odor of oil burning and garbage rotting seeps in. I wonder how any life could exist there, noting how ironic it is that these places sustain life everywhere else.

The old lady next to me moves in her sleep, unfolding her arms to reveal a Florida vacation planner. I imagine not stopping in Princeton and heading for Florida and the beaches with palm trees and the 100 percent humidity to keep the skin young. I would become someone else, someone tan, someone aloof who sits on the beach all day ignoring everything and everyone except for the sun. A passing train lays in on its whistle. The old lady jerks in a sort of hiccuping motion that is frightening to see. Closing my eyes, the whole Florida scene plays before me. The waves tumble against the white sand, while the wings of stingrays flap just above the surface of the salty water. I walk into the water anyway, looking behind me at the beach, finding no one to stop me from going any farther.

"Princeton Junction," a metallic voice from above

announces. My eyes pass quickly over the vacation planner, but I leave my seat and continue forward through the doors, which close immediately behind me as I step out onto the platform. I think about calling my mother to come pick me up. There is no guarantee that Ruby is even home; I didn't call first. I walk across the station and decide to wait for the Dingy to take me home.

But home really isn't Princeton. Princeton belongs to Allen, Ruby's fourth husband, the macroeconomics professor. He is overseas this month for a conference, and Ruby canceled her ticket because of my wedding. This was shocking, but I think it also had more to do with the conference being in South Africa than it had to do with my wedding.

Ruby wasn't a hands-on mother. If there was someplace better to be, she would go, no matter what milestone of my life she was missing. She missed my high school graduation and the opening night to the first gallery exhibit of my photography. She was even out on some ranch in the middle of nowhere when one of my photos made the cover of the *New York Times*. It was probably the only place on earth that didn't sell the *Times*. And she would dismiss her absence with an upward wave of her manicured hand and a souvenir from wherever she and the new man-husband went. A shell necklace from Bali, a miniature bottle of Chanel No. 5 from the Charles de Gaulle duty-free shop, and a shot glass from that ranch with a gunshot right through the middle of it.

The Dingy whistles and hoots itself up to the platform, all the doors popping open to release two kids with skateboards and the conductor, who saunters slowly with a wide hip swing over to the main station building like some kind of male supermodel. I decide to wait for him to come back before stepping onto the train. The Dingy isn't like the trains coming from New York. This is more like a school bus, and in some sense, I guess it is. Ruby bragged to me about it in her first letters from Princeton. They have their own train, she said, all to their little selves. She was really taken with the place, and now, with fallen leaves everywhere in huge orange, brown, and red piles, I can't blame her. The conductor returns, crunching boldly over the fallen leaves on the platform, coffee and *New York Times* in hand. He tips his hat at me and enters into his little officelike space. We speed over the highway, what once was a farm, and onto the campus with its antique train station.

The university looks so peaceful and so quiet, like a person could really concentrate on things, but I don't trust it as I step off the train. I look up into the empty windows that reflect the white puffs of clouds in the sky, and it all seems too perfect. It is as though a photographer rolled through a few minutes before I arrived and arranged the cumulus in the best puffy way, called the birds to silence, and paid off the skateboarders to go play somewhere else. I walk tentatively toward the sidewalk like a cat on a damp floor, waiting for the scene to give like a papier-mâché set for a children's play. A distant streetlight proceeds through its pattern, no cars coming in either direction.

I walk toward Nassau, trying to remember which path heads to Allen's house and, hopefully, Ruby, not wanting to walk in circles. Leaves crushed brown, yellow, and orange lie on the still-green grass. The little train slowly pushes itself away from the platform. Canada geese flap quietly overhead, creating a small disturbance to the leaves. I look up in the too-blue sky to watch them pass. Heaven, to me, used to be the sky. After my father died, people assured me that he was watching me. Watching you from above, they said, and I took it literally. I would spend hours in the backyard of my grandparents' house staring at the sky, expecting the sun or the stars to wink at me or spell out some secret message from my dad.

I stop at the front gate of the college and look up at the sky, which is framed on either side by autumn oak trees. A huge pillow of a cloud drifts quietly over the sun. After a few minutes, two gauzy rays poke holes through the cloud. In those beams, I find hope; the hope I need to brace myself from the storm of Ruby's reaction to the news of my wedding. Allen's offer to take her to

South Africa will seem like a much better deal now. And I can't imagine her not being afraid to tell me so.

Nassau Street reminds me of Hoboken a little with all the small shops and people bustling around like they have someplace important to be. Drew was an ace at that type of walking. Maybe it came from being on Wall Street. When he took to the streets, it was like some winged furies took over his feet and sped him about, head held high, arms swinging boldly at either side. He looked like an Armani ad, his suit freshly dry-cleaned, the brown spikes of his hair neatly gelled into place, his chin residing in some no-stubble zone. I loved that look of determination and success, and I was especially drawn to his. To me, he was pure energy. It was like that when he rode his bikes, too. He became a blur, whizzing by like a bird swooping down briefly before returning to the sky. He became one with the movement and disappeared into it.

Slowing down, I watch these people pass. I close my eyes and imagine that the breeze created in their wake isn't theirs at all but Drew's. Stopping in the middle of the sidewalk, I open my arms a little wider to catch more of the familiar sensation. I take in so much of it that I am fooled and believe for a split second that it is indeed him. Looking up I find a woman with a deluxe mountain-climbing stroller hustling ahead of me.

I turn down a quiet side street, grateful to be away

from the morning walkers and their gathering of bagels and newspapers. My mother's front door appears, looking like something out of calendar titled "The Front Doors of America." A dried floral wreath blocks most of the door and matches the trim on the shutters, the flowers planted along the walkway, and in the mailbox planter. I step onto the porch with every intention of knocking on the door. Instead, I turn and sit. The slippery fresh paint of the porch steps feels cool under my sweaty palms. A breeze blows down the street, creating little tornadoes of leaves that rush around and under my mother's Honda. They sound like the rush of children's footsteps, scurrying off to do something they probably shouldn't.

Fishing an old cigarette out of the pocket of my coat, I notice the shaking of my hands. I hold them out in front of me and watch them wobble, doing nothing to stop it. I can see that they are shaking, but I can't feel it. I put the cigarette back, not wanting to disturb the feeling, and lean back against the porch steps, closing my eyes. Am I allowed to have a big, white dress? Should I order a cake with tiers and flowers? Would anyone come? Is my mother going to help me? Turning from the sound of my own voice in my head, I listen instead to a flock of Canada geese call and bark overhead. Eager noises from beings intent on getting where they need to go. I open my eyes and watch the geese escape out of sight. If only I could have been so intent. If only I had seen winter coming and done more to be prepared.

"They must be practicing," Ruby says, startling me completely.

"Mom," I start to say, looking at this woman in a red terry robe and holding a big cup of coffee sitting next to me, a woman I would not have recognized as my mother. "You own a robe?" I ask, taking the cigarette back out and lighting it up. "A terry-cloth robe?" Ruby was always one for the finer things. This attitude plus the constant flow of boyfriends and husbands kept Ruby's appearance in check. She was never one to let her face be seen without makeup or her hair undone. Appearance, she would say to me, is everything.

"Hannah, of course I own a robe, everyone does," she says, as if everyone made everything all right. Yeah, I wish.

"But on the porch?"

"You don't seem to have a problem with the porch, and why are you still smoking. After all that's happened, you think smoking is okay. Do you want to have a heart attack, too?"

"Sometimes," I say, letting the idea of dying right on this porch roll around in my mind before resting my chin on my knees to stop them from shaking. "I want to talk to you about the wedding."

A car drives by, honking twice, and Ruby waves back

like a prom queen. "A neighbor," she says. "I wanted to ask you about that, did you guys pay for the reception hall, if so, Allen says you can demand a refund, but that you best do on Monday. You really don't want all that money going to waste. And you need to cancel the minister and what else wasn't included in the package?"

I refuse to answer and look away. I try blowing the smoke from my cigarette into the wind. It rushes back into my face. I hide a cough in the sleeve of my polar fleece pullover.

"Okay then, what is it you want to talk about?" Ruby asks, adjusting the red terry cloth around her ankles, trying to look official and together on her front porch. She leans over and picks a short brown curl of hair off my shoulder. She holds it by two fingers, dangling it in front of us, before dropping it into the wind. The strand of hair disappears in seconds. Drew's hair. I look over the lawn, which undulates in the breeze. A little piece of him propelled by an unseen force now navigates my mother's lawn. There must be thousands of little pieces of him all over our unkempt apartment, surrounding me and everything that was once ours. There must be pieces of him everywhere, moving without being seen throughout the world.

"Where does it all go?" Ruby says.

The breeze dies down and the grass unfolds itself back toward us. I don't know where it all goes, and I don't want to know. I would much rather have it all back. "We haven't got a minister yet," I say.

"Good, that's one less thing to do. Come on in, lemme make you some breakfast."

"I'm going through with it," I blurt out quickly, bringing my knees closer to my chest, throwing the cigarette to the ground. Its red ember tip flares up slightly, then fades to gray and dies out on the concrete walk.

I see thoughts turning in her mind and brace myself for her response. She puts her hands on either side of her head and sighs. I wasn't expecting that.

"I should have done this months ago," I stammer, hoping to get some kind of response from her.

Quietly she asks me, "What makes you think doing something as outlandish as this will rectify what you should have done months ago?"

My defenses are triggered instantly, despite her quiet tones. "Outlandish?" I shout as I stand up; the leaves gathered at the base of the porch painfully snap and crunch.

"Hannah, sit down. Drew died, and you didn't plan that. Talk to me." Ruby folds her arms across her chest.

"You know I didn't even have a damn dress. And I don't even know where the banquet place is. He booked it."

"What's this thing gonna prove?"

"That I wanted it. That I was wrong. Don't you

remember saying to me that my father was with you for weeks after he died, that you felt him? Well, I feel like Drew is still with me, and this is how I can show him. Prove my love to him." I pull my hands quickly out of my coat pockets. The old pack of cigarettes settles lifelessly on the ground.

Ruby picks up my pack of cigarettes, turning it around a few times, before taking one out and lighting it. She inhales deeply and exhales the smoke into a single ribbon that stretches out above her head. Everything she did was first rate. Everything except for me.

"Just how do you expect to proceed from here?"

"I'm going to call everyone—"

"What?" Ruby asks.

"Call them, the guests, tell them—"

"Tell them what? Tell them that you are marrying a dead man because you still feel him." Ruby stubs out the cigarette in the cement landing, burning a small hole through one of the dried leaves. "Believe me, sweetheart, I speak from personal experience, mention that once and people will treat you like a crazy person for years. Remember after your father died?"

And I remember my dad's funeral, and the way her friends and the women in the family hovered around her but not near her, as if she had the flu or pneumonia, something treatable but possibly still contagious. I can still picture her with her head down on the kitchen table like one of my first-grade classmates during story time. She kept talking, not to the women around her, but to my father. She said his name over and over again, calling out like he was just in the backyard taking too long to get inside for supper.

"Fine, then I'll say it's a money thing, that we already paid for it, and that Drew wouldn't want it to be wasted."

"And they'll buy that? His parents, the ever awful Mr. and Mrs. Heinz?" Ruby asks, shaking her head, already discounting the Heinzes' power of imagination and capacity to accept.

"Well, I don't know about that yet. I'll send them a note. Something respectful. It's almost been a month."

"Hannah, what are you doing to these people?"

"It can't be what am I doing to people, it's what am I doing for me. I can't run around with this fear that he's watching me, thinking that I never gave a damn, that I lied to him." I stop to take a breath and to stop myself from sounding like a moron on a soap. She didn't get it, and I couldn't explain it. Marriage was going to change everything, and that was one fact of life I never wanted to experience firsthand. I didn't want to lose the way our life was for the sake of some big party and a notarized piece of paper.

I exhale forcefully, sit up straight. "And I'm not asking

you for advice. I'm asking you to help me and be my friend and take me to get a damn dress."

Ruby stands, tightening the strap of her robe. "Come inside. I need more coffee for this."

I hold open the screen door as she scoops the newspaper up off the front mat, which matches the autumn tones in the wreath, the landscaping, and the trim on the house. "You need coffee for this," I say under my breath.

The inside of Ruby's house surprises me because it actually looks like she lives there now. Allen's first wife died in this house, and when Ruby moved in, she was reluctant to even change the color of a bath mat. She put her things in storage, not wanting to disrupt Allen. When she told me this, I almost choked on my club sandwich. But obviously something has changed.

Her collection of ducks rests in the built-in next to the television table, about thirty of them in wood, ceramic, glass, colorful and plain, comical and natural. We had those very same ducks in the front windowsill of our house in Hartford, the kitchen china cupboard in Westchester, and on the coffee table in Morristown, but if you were to take these ducks to a church rummage sale, I would have never been able to distinguish which ones were ours. I stand with the ducks, listening to Ruby bang the coffee-filter basket against the countertop or the side of the trash can. I pick them up one by one, trying to memorize the feel of them, the looks on their little painted and carved faces.

Ruby steps out of the kitchen, oddly dressed now in jeans and a sweatshirt with flowers embroidered on it to match her sneakers; I hadn't heard her go upstairs and change. I want to ask her what they did with my mother, but she hands me coffee, with just enough milk, in my favorite mug with the wisteria-vine handle, so I don't. I want things to go smoothly. I want her help. "So," I say, "whereabouts do you think we could find a dress?"

She places her quickly emptied cup down on the console table, completely disregarding the coasters, and says to me without missing a beat, "Don't worry about it, I know just the place." She smiles, her lipstick spreading out a little into the fjords around her lips.

For a Sunday, making it to the Turnpike is a smooth ride. Ruby drives quickly, making turns without asking for directions, grabbing the ticket from the toll taker and speeding off southbound. I don't think to ask where we're headed. I just rest my head on the window, letting everything familiar fly by.

Ruby and I used to drive a lot of places when I was younger between moving, visiting my grandparents, and vacationing with the many stepfathers and the boyfriends in between. I tried to stay awake and take in all the sights, but everything moved too fast for me. After about fifty miles, I can't look out the window anymore. The changing scenery is just too much for me. I prefer to see life in snapshots, fixed moments that you can study, savor, and count on being right where you left them.

Drew and I hadn't been on the Turnpike since he started training stockbroker wanna-bes to take the Series 7 exams. All his free time went into preparing his classes and making up the lost time at his regular job. The terrain has changed since then. New developments of town homes and condos spring up around every exit. When they first started building town homes near our favorite grocery store, Drew asked me, with complete seriousness, where all the people came from.

"They moved here," I said with a little too much of a tone in my voice, irritated at always having to know the answers, "like you did, where's the great mystery?"

"Well, yeah. I just wanted to know what you thought." He stared straight out the window, rapidly changing lanes to get around a semi and a Ford Taurus. He turned up the radio too loud, and I knew I had hurt his feelings. He was one of those people who genuinely wanted to know things, and not just about a few subject areas, about everything. If we drove past a chicken-processing factory, he wanted to know about chicken consumption; if we flew over a naval yard on our way to the Bahamas, he wondered how many men were stationed there with families. Drew was naturally curious, a gossip even.

"Look at that," I said to him, pointing out a nice end unit with a patio set and a huge gas grill on the deck. "Those people there, you know, the Thompsons, they had to move from the city because the upstairs neighbors were real vegan types and couldn't stand the smell of London broil on the grill. The deck only made sense."

And then he laughed. And laughed. Laughed for what seemed like the rest of the day, pumping me for more information about the Thompsons, about why they got married, if they liked their jobs, if they drove a foreign or American car.

I look over at Ruby, who is intensely studying the names of the cities on the exit about to come up, wanting to tell her about Drew and the Thompsons. Her hands tight around the steering wheel, her knuckles whiten. I want to tell her about the patio set, and the way Drew sounded when he was happy.

"Mom," I say.

She tries to smile. "I'm lost."

"Lost?" I ask. This used to be a problem with my mother trying out shortcuts to get to places she thought she wanted to go or remembered having been before.

"Need exit three, but I'm not sure if I want A or B."

"Three doesn't have an A or B, it's just exit three."

She loosens her grip on the steering wheel. "Whew, I didn't want to worry you."

She reaches out and pinches my waist. I used to love that, but I always squirmed and wiggled, trying to get away from her. Never too far, though, always close enough that she could reach.

"No worries," I say.

"Really? Not even about this thing?" Ruby asks, turning her head to change lanes. She signals after she's in the right lane.

"Don't call it 'this thing.'"

"Whaddaya want me to call it? Hard enough as is without having to argue about what to call it?"

"We're not arguing." I throw my head back against the headrest of the seat. My neck aches from dozing off on the train and a knot ties up the right side of my shoulder. My display of emotion doesn't help. "There's your exit," I say, moving my hand to point it out as she accelerates toward the ramp. My hand hits the window, and I decide it is useless to define it. Or argue with Ruby about it. Whatever *it* is.

Just beyond the exit by about two lights is Samuel's House of Brides. Brides and bridesmaids swarm about the parking lot and race into the store to find the many dresses advertised marked down from five hundred dollars to fifty. They advertise like Crazy Eddie's used to, only instead of Crazy Eddie, they have the Chaotic Bride. Only five thousand, only five thousand, she shouts, picking up the tags to dress after dress in a fancy department store, a salesman in an overly fashionable suit stands next to her, pencil behind his ear, financing brochure in hand. Then, magic bubbles float over the edges of the screen. The camera angle pulls up, and we see the bride at Samuel's. Only five thousand, she says again, only five thousand dresses to choose from. Then the words Do It Right! flash up and the picture of the chaotic bride fades. Drew's sister, Miranda, used to joke about taking me here.

"I don't think this is the right place," I tell Ruby as she pulls into a parking space. "I don't really think Samuel's will have the right thing for the nonbride."

A group of four girls bounce into the front doors of the store.

"I see why you would say that, but aren't you the least bit curious?"

"This is crazy. I said I needed *a* dress, not *the* dress."

"I know what you said, and you said you were going through with the wedding. You didn't mention anything else about how you may or may not do it."

"Ruby."

She looks over at me, head tilted slightly to the side, eyes narrowing in on me, a truly interested and concerned glance. "You used to love this stuff."

And I did, a long time ago when all my older cousins got married in big princess-style gowns with veils and trains and attendants. I was even flower girl a few times. But now?

"A real dress?" I ask.

"Who's to say you can't?"

Inside the store, past the racks of dresses arranged by color and length, stand more brides than I could count, perched on pale pink carpeted pedestals, their attendants and mothers circling around them holding up this veil and that headpiece, or another dress with the perfect sleeves or the best bodice yet. Rena, my best friend from work, almost got married once. She took me to a few dress stores and wouldn't try anything on. *I just don't see it yet,* she said to me, later breaking off the wedding for much the same reason. Thumbing through the racks of pink taffeta, I try to see it. The banquet hall all done in flowers and tea lights. Flowers in my hair to match the ones embroidered on the organza of my dress. Relatives dancing drunkenly to "Celebration" by Kool and the Gang.

"Organza," I tell my mother. "Tea-length with flowers embroidered around the hem or maybe the bodice, I don't know, just organza I guess, definitely not white."

"I love that," she says. "What a perfect idea. I think I saw a lovely one with a floral, lacy bodice in candlelight."

Having been married so many times Ruby was very good at finding the right dress for touchy situations. And not always for herself. A few of the older cousins were having the proverbial shotgun wedding, and even then only after things became more apparent than is usually fashionable in uptight New England towns. Ruby invariably found the right dress to complement both the girl's height and widening girth. When I got older and started taking pictures of these glorious events, you couldn't even detect a slight bulge.

"Would you like to try something on?" the salesgirl asks, mumbling really, as Ruby thrusts several dresses past me and into her hands.

"She'll try those," Ruby says. "I'll need some help buttoning her into the one with the lace top. Arthritis makes mother-of-pearl so difficult. Go, go."

She pushes me toward the girl, tripping me against the pedestal that is now mine, and into an overly pink dressing room with a plush carpet. The few stains on the carpet below me instantly ruin the posh effect as I step into the first dress. My first wedding dress.

The first one is beyond reason. High neck, long sleeves, full skirt with what feels like fifty yards of crinoline that scratches against my thighs as I step out of the dressing room to be buttoned in. The little satin-covered buttons pinch as the salesgirl closes them from my ass to the top of my neck. She seems to carry straight pins in her mouth at all times, mumbling up to me when she is done buttoning something that sounds like "Is that all right?" Does she forget to take them out at the end of the night and go home to her unsuspecting boyfriend and kiss him, stabbing him brutally? Or did he learn to remind her about the pins before he got into stabbing range or does he leave sticky notes in her car telling her to spit them out before she gets in?

"Isn't that tough to hold pins in your mouth?" I ask, letting my curiosity get the better of me.

"Easier," she answers, whacking at the faded beige skirt until all the folds are symmetrical.

"Mom," I say, stepping onto the pedestal in front of the three-sided mirror, "do you honestly think this is the way to go here? I mean, it is beige, but we're not talking so formal here are we?"

Tears slip down Ruby's cheeks as she shifts the slight train of the dress to my left side. "It's just so, so pretty and I knew even if you did do the whole thing you never would have gotten into something like this."

"Don't take advantage and quit crying." I avoid looking at myself, not wanting to get attached, but my eyes fixate against my better judgment on the perfectly symmetrical folds that surround what now looks to be my dainty waist. I can see this, but not for the future as it now stands. Sheer temptation prompts me to spin once in a circle. The skirt swishes effortlessly back into place.

I shake my head at the pin-mouth lady, and she unbuttons me quickly, shoving me back into the dressing room faster than I expected. I listen to a new group of bridesmaids shout questions over the racks of gowns to the pin-mouth lady. Questions about green velvet and April weddings.

Velvet has a nice touch to it, but it would be much too heavy for April, I think to myself. "Too warm for the church," I yell over the dressing-room door.

"Yeah," they said in almost unison. "See, Allison. No velvet."

For a minute I regret shooting down Allison's plans, it being her wedding and all, but torturing people for your own sake isn't very nice. And then I realize people could say I'm doing the same thing.

"A pastel velvet would be nice," I yell over again. "A light purple maybe, like frost on crocus buds."

"I love crocus buds," a girl, maybe Allison, with a thick, almost midwestern accent, says. "Is there any purple velvet?" I smile, listening to the footsteps of the group pad off toward the front of the store.

The next dress isn't as heavy as the first. In fact, it is much lighter than it looks. It flutters over my head before slipping down over my shoulders. A butter-cream yellow number with a chiffon tea-length skirt and bodice with a long-sleeved yellow lace jacket that opens in the back, closing with a bow the same color and material as the skirt. I move around, shifting myself and the dress in the mirror. Try my hair up. Try my hair down. Sit down on the chair and cross my legs. Cross them the other way. I stand up, unable to take my eyes off the dress. Off me in the dress.

I slowly open the dressing-room door, looking cautiously each way.

"Well," Ruby says. "That's from the twenty-five-off rack, you know."

The skirt swirls around me as I slip out of the dressing room and walk out toward the pedestal. I can almost hear the tapping of high heels on a dance floor.

"That's a real waltzer of a dress," Ruby says, drawing in a deep breath.

The five purple bridesmaids escorted by Allison return with mounds of gowns draped over their arms. "Look how perfect that hem falls," Allison says. "Beautiful," the five purple bridesmaids say, as the group shuffles past me to the back of the dressing-room area.

"And it's yours, Hannah. Take it off and let's go before we make a mistake and not take it."

I want to stand on the pedestal a little longer. I want to stare at myself in this dress, burn the impression in my mind. I would like to remember what this actually feels like, as opposed to what it should have felt like. The pin-mouth lady pushes me back into my dressing room to make room for the purple-velvet-clad troupe emerging from the large dressing room in the back. I stand in the dressing room, spin around a few times, and watch the hem flare up and around like a child's Fourth of July pin-wheel. Dizziness sets in, and it feels good to be dizzy, to be a little off balance.

When I was a kid I couldn't even hula-hoop because it made me dizzy, and I hated that. I never liked that out-of-control frenzy you needed to maintain to keep the hoop up in a proper place. But now, I take pleasure in the dizziness, realizing that I have spent countless days with my teeth clenched, trying to fight off every and all emotions. I spin until I have to sit down, the beautiful chiffon spreading around me like a glowing, alien orb.

Ruby knocks on the hollow door to my dressing room a few times. "Yeah," I say.

Nothing comes from the other side of the door for a few minutes. "Yeah," I say again, only a little louder.

"You okay?"

I'm not sure how to answer that. I look down at the chiffon billowing up around me and my jeans and sweat-shirt strewn about the floor like debris in some Victorian painting that makes a statement about decadence. My art history professor would be proud. Even in the middle of adversity, art is everywhere you look for it. "Maybe," I say.

"Okay, then, well, maybe you want to sit there awhile, collect yourself, relax."

I know instantly that she is hiding something from me. I stand tiptoe to look over the door. Allison, in full bridal splendor, is standing on my pedestal. The purple-clad attendants circle and swarm around like bugs from the tropical rain forest. Her mother weeps openly in the gilded Louis XIV chair off to the side. Allison's skirt not only billows, it explodes with shocking white tulle, briefly interrupted by what looks to be hand-embroidered roses. Her plain satin bodice is accentuated when the tallest of the purple-clad girls, with fiery red hair that falls in huge curls down her back, fastens a three-strand pearl choker around Allison's dainty neck. "Isn't She Lovely" by Stevie Wonder filters in through the Muzak system, and I agree for one of the few times in my life that my mother is right. I need to sit down and try not to think too much about this.

"Gimme the dress," Ruby says.

Without protest, I slip the dress off over my head and hand it to her. She reaches over the top of the door and takes the hanger. I sink back down in just my underwear, unable to focus on my thoughts. I pull on my sweatshirt to keep from being cold and hum along with Stevie Wonder. Allison's bridal party giddily shouts in unison, "She'll take it!" And I listen to the whole group gallop off to their dressing rooms. I quickly tug on my jeans, hoping to escape without being a part of their happiness.

Ruby is standing in front of the Wall of Brides, a photo monument to all the women who bought their bridal attire at the store. She points out a picture the size of a pizza box. The picture is full of people, with six bridesmaids and groomsmen in addition to three flower girls and ring bearers. The crowd of guests behind them was equally large.

"It was like that when I married your father," she said, surprising me because I don't ever remember pictures the size of pizza boxes from their wedding. I actually don't remember seeing any pictures from their wedding.

"Really?" I ask, not wanting to ask after pictures that might be a sore subject.

"He was friends with everybody. You should have seen the crowd." Ruby looks off toward the pictures but not at them for a few minutes before turning to me. "You ready?"

"Yeah," I say, slipping the dress hanger off her finger. "Lemme carry it."

For all the brides and bridesmaids in the store, the checkout stand is surprisingly quick. After two troupes of at least five maids and a bride, the cashier smiles brightly at me and asks, "Everything okay?"

I don't have the heart to say no, so I just nod at her as she searches the layers of chiffon and lace for a price tag.

"That's from the twenty-five off," Ruby adds, leaning over my shoulder.

"Everything is," the girl says flatly. She taps a finger against the counter while her computer searches for the price for the control number she punched in. The tips of her pink fingernails are chipped. "Five hundred, twenty-six," she finally says with a sigh.

"What?" I say, raising my voice instantly. What happened to the fifty dollars they advertised?

"Five hundred and twenty-six dollars," she says, fast-forwarding the receipt. "Yep, the twenty-five percent off was already deducted." She extends the register tape to me and points with a chewed nail at the reduction in red ink on the tape.

"What about all these signs saying dresses are fifty dollars?"

Nail-polish girl turns her head and nods at a rack of Miss America dresses size 24 in the far corner of the store. It is an explosion of sequins and diamonique spangles. "You gotta read the signs," she says.

I take a deep breath, not wanting to explode all at once. Before I can get the first word out, Ruby slips her American Express card across to the girl. The plastic bends back and snaps against the counter as she picks it up. "Cool, a hologram," she says, handing the card and the receipt back to Ruby. Another girl with a pink button that reads Manager drags my dress across the counter and zips it into a pink opaque bag before I can say or do anything else.

I can't take my eyes off the bag; Ruby's signature billows in the breeze on the receipt taped to the hook of the hanger. Ruby watches me staring at the bag as she opens the trunk to her Honda. "It won't fade in the bag," she says, as if that is enough to explain away my confusion with the transaction that just occurred.

Ruby drives slowly back to Princeton, staying off the Turnpike, sticking to little country roads that roll and dip, the kind of roads children with strong stomachs love.

"Did I have a strong stomach as a kid?" I ask.

"Do you mean, did you throw up a lot? No more so than most children. I was reading this study in one of Allen's journals about the economic success factors in marketing children's medical products to an overafraid—"

"You've been living in a university town too long, it's gone to your head."

"Well," Ruby says, pursing her lips together, "something besides champagne had to eventually. And I like it there. Everyone has their lawn cut, all the time, and if not, the looks will fly."

"Really, that's no good reason to like a place because the people are pretentious."

"It's not pretense, it's standards. The whole place kind of expects more of you, and I need that. Order and sensibility."

Sounds like a Victorian novel, I think, carefully avoiding saying it and ruining the few nice moments we had together today. She takes a left and another left, putting us on a street that looks like another movie set, this time for small-town America circa 1954. The leaves from all the lawns are in neat piles along the curbs. Old men with hats shuffling along the streets in pairs. Overgrown children walk dogs on long leashes. Pumpkins glow not-so-scary grins at passersby. Amazed, I try to take it all in, wishing that I remembered my camera. I suddenly feel lost without it. I would want a close-up of an almost ghoulish pumpkin, something I could double-expose over a nice happy street scene with dogs in sweaters.

"Drew," I start to say, wanting to bounce the idea off of him, to hear him laugh at me.

"Yes, what about Drew?" Ruby asks briefly, in between humming along with the oldies station.

"Nothing," I say, heat rising up into my cheeks, realizing I didn't want to talk about him to Ruby or anyone else. I wanted to keep to myself the way he would lean over me, resting his chin on my shoulder, fingering my hair, as he studied whatever print I asked him to. After a while he would sigh, flatten his lips into a frown, and tell me how wonderful my work was and that even if he had all the money in the world, it still wouldn't be enough to buy such a piece of art. I wanted to keep moments like those safely inside, someplace inescapable and mine.

She smiles at me and pulls into a parking lot next to a large Victorian house with enough porch for an entire retirement community.

"I thought you should eat. I know you don't feel

hungry, but you really should eat. You'll feel better and this place has great tea." Ruby turns the car off and puts her hand on my knee. "Please, just a little."

I didn't think I was protesting, so I just nod.

The restaurant is one of those places that prides itself on gravy and mashed potatoes, and I think it is odd that Ruby would even know about such a place, let alone frequent it. The gingerbread trim was done in white, lavender, sky blue, and pink. A pink neon sign in an antique wrought-iron grill advertises Home Cooking to passersby on the road. She holds the door open for me, and we are immediately greeted by a woman in a floor-length floral gown with a starched white full-front apron.

"What's your pleasure?" Aunt Bea asks in the worst southern accent attempted. "Smokin' or no."

I turn to look at Ruby. "Smoking," she says, putting a hand on my shoulder.

"You eat here?" I ask. "You?"

"Allen loves it. And the sweet-potato pie is divine. Absolute food for the soul."

I try to picture my mother and economist Allen in a real soul-food joint in someplace like Harlem. Ruby wearing some kind of tight-fitting nylon dress that makes her look busty with the top button undone, her legs wrapped sexily around Allen and his khakis. This thought shakes from my head when Ruby grabs a cigarette from my hand and lights it for herself.

"What's up with you?" I ask.

"I'm worried."

"Why, what's wrong with Allen?"

She places the cigarette in the ashtray that is still full from the last customers. Her lipstick marks the tip like blood. "Not Allen, you. What are you doing this for?"

"I already told you." I watch Aunt Bea circling the room with a pitcher of iced tea, wishing she would let us order some. I feel like I am about to cry. Or maybe scream.

"Fine then, how do you plan on getting this done? What are you going to do?"

"I don't know," I said, raising my cracking voice. "I don't know yet. Where's the fucking waitress?"

"Hannah."

"Mom."

The statute of limitations for our getting along expires as the waitress, dressed very similar to Aunt Bea only with a shorter skirt, waddles over to take our cholesterol-laden order. We each order the meat loaf special with honey carrots and mashed potatoes.

"Extra gravy," Ruby says.

Aunt Bea number two looks at me.

I nod, handing her both sticky menus.

This is normal, though, us eating without talking. I was actually used to it by the time I got to college. The dining hall weirded me out with everyone sitting together and talking, giving me indigestion before I chewed my first bite. I got over it, though, and never expected to be sharing a meal with someone who wouldn't speak to me ever again.

"Nice dress, isn't it?" I ask, looking up over my meat loaf at Ruby, who is still busy slicing hers into little gravy-coated morsels.

"Yeah," she says, sticking equal portions of meat loaf and mashed potatoes into her mouth. She looks away, out toward the parking lot, and the few cars that pass on the street. She eats more carrots. More potatoes and meat. Settles her napkin down on the table and sighs.

I decide to leave it at that. No need to change things now. I could feel Drew's fingers on my shoulder, squeezing in a rhythmic pattern to let me know it was okay to drop the whole thing. He was good like that. A mediator. *Pick your battles,* he said to me, *know what it's worth before you start.* I want to turn around and hear him say it to me, watch his lips form the quieting words, but there is no one standing over my shoulder. No one to look at or talk to or feel touching me. My throat pinches sharply in the back, and a long swallow of iced tea does more harm than good. My head begins to throb, and I want Ruby to say something, to do something.

"I'm not feeling well," I say. "My throat and my head."

"Aspirin? Think I have some." Ruby snaps open her purse and pokes around before producing a bottle with three aspirin left.

I take all three and leave the bottle on the table. "Thanks," I say, fingering the empty bottle on the table, imagining for a moment that they weren't really aspirin at all but something deadly. Arsenic tablets. I am going to die, I think, growing comfortable with the idea. I settle back in my chair, close my eyes, and wait, but nothing happens.

Ruby counts over some crumpled bills for the check and stands up, her jeans wrinkled with a little gravy stain on the left thigh. This couldn't be her. The Ruby I remembered wouldn't eat gravy, be stained by food, or for that matter wear jeans into a restaurant. It must be me, I think, suddenly feeling very guilty for making her worry. I never wanted to hurt anyone else. Especially not her, especially not after what she did for me today. "You know, if you really think this is a bad idea, I won't."

Ruby puts the keys in the ignition but stops before turning them. "I can't say that I don't think this is the most outlandish thing I've ever heard of, but what happened to This Is What I Have to Do?"

I reach over and turn the keys in the ignition, before

turning to face the window. All the food in my stomach makes me feel suddenly tired, and I can't think straight. *I just don't want anyone to be hurt anymore,* I say silently to myself.

Ruby doesn't move to put the car in gear. "Hannah, I asked you a question."

"Drop it. Please." My voice cracks on the *please,* and Ruby places a hand on my shoulder, rubbing it a few times, before putting the car in gear and pulling out of the parking lot.

When I wake up, we are pulling into Allen's driveway. No lights are on in the house, and I forget for a minute that Allen is in South Africa trying to save the world via his Economic Theory of Global Markets. I don't want to spend the night here, and I know that I could say no and get on the train. If I was asked, I could say no. But Ruby won't ask. She'll simply expect me to be staying the night.

Ruby gets out of the car, taking the dress with her into the house. I follow slowly behind, still not quite awake. The grass is damp and spongy under my feet. The streetlights pop on one after another in a procession down the street. I forgot how dark it can be outside of Hoboken. And how quiet. I stop on the front porch to listen to the sounds of nothing and think for the first time that it might be okay to stay here for a few days, that it might help to be somewhere peaceful.

My Intended

"Mom," I call out, stepping into the house, "is the bed in the guest room made? I'd like to stay."

"Of course it's made, and of course you'll stay," Ruby answers, sticking her head into the living room briefly. I listen to the muffled voices coming from the answering machine, wishing that one of them was for me. I hear Allen send love, love, love, love and kisses, kisses, kisses, to his wife, wife, wife, causing me to suddenly revoke my wish to be in that house as I realize that my mother will always be somebody's wife.

The stairs are carpeted in a thick heavy plush that made your feet feel ten thousand times heavier than they really are. I tug myself using the handrail, avoiding the smiling faces of Allen's three boys that line the hallway. They are all older than me and live in Madrid, Tokyo, and Stockholm. The two oldest sons didn't even show up for Allen and Ruby's wedding; they sent plane tickets so Allen and Ruby could visit them in London or Florence instead. Ruby decided that made his sons less than thoughtful. And she wasn't afraid to say something about it to anyone within earshot. I can't bear the thought that Ruby or anyone else might think less of me because of going through with this wedding. I resent the sons' wide-gapped smiles now more than ever and am grateful that the pictures stop at the door to the master bedroom and don't continue down to the door of the guest room.

The guest room is a lavender paradise with subtle floral wallpaper and plush carpet the color of spring hyacinth. Slipping off my shoes as I sink into the down comforter, I let the whole room well up around me like water in the pool. I try to think about my dress and the sounds of dancing feet on wooden floors, the sound of Drew sharing jokes with me under his breath at the altar. I try to think about our wedding, the one that should have been and not the one yet to come.

Saturday, April 18, 1979

In the morning, the downstairs kitchen table, instead of
being set with two bowls, two spoons, and a box of
Raisin Bran—the breakfast we always had—a crushed
box of Krispy Kreme doughnuts sat, jelly gushing out
like guts. The kitchen floor was cold under my bare feet,
but my mom wasn't around to make the dog tell where
he hid my slippers. She was upstairs, bathroom door
locked, with Louis's sisters, Marlene and Kate. I heard
them laughing as I walked past. Their lipstick, a cheap
whore red as my mom once called it, stained the cigarette butts in the ashtray next to the box of doughnuts. I
poured myself a glass of milk and stepped out into the
backyard to watch the tent.

The tent probably amazed me most. In what used to
be our backyard, in the place where my dad sunk the

ends of my swing set in old paint cans filled with concrete, there was a tent, all white, with little white chairs and tables underneath. Caterers scurried from the truck and back with platters of luncheon meat and shrimp cocktail. Enough for a hundred people. Louis's people. My mom wasn't even inviting Grandmom; she'd had her wedding, and this one was all Louis. At least that's what she said. Louis didn't seem to care too much and had been out on the road promoting some new talent the last two weeks. Cincinnati, St. Louis, and beyond, he said, as he kissed Mom on the cheek and banged his ratty suitcase on the doorframe my dad let me paint last summer.

The main event, Marlene's words, was set to begin in about an hour, and I knew I should slip on my dress, the one I wear to Sunday school, and be ready for when people get here. I wasn't wearing pink or satin or walking down the aisle with the bridal party. It was my job to take the pictures with the stupid camera Kate brought over a couple of weeks ago. Louis thought it was a great idea since they couldn't find a real photographer on short notice, and the pictures would look good in his promo pack. He threw his saggy arm around my mom and said, *Everyone loves a family man.* If that was true, why wasn't I included, I wanted to say, but at that point I didn't care. If Marlene and Kate wanted to wear those stupid gowns that made more noise than a swarm of bees when they walked, then they could have them. They could keep being family for the family man, and I would just be me.

Upstairs again, past the door of cackling hyenas and some nose-burning smell, I slipped on my Sunday dress, not caring if it needed to be ironed a little more around the hem. I brushed my hair back as best I could and snapped barrettes behind each of my ears. My mom wasn't around to tell me not to, so I pulled out my summer sandals, the ones with heart-shaped cutouts, and put them on without socks even though I knew the grass would still be cold and wet.

In the hallway, I tromped around a bit, making a lot of noise to try and get their attention. I stopped. Waited. But no one opened the door. With a loud sigh, I headed downstairs to the living room to wait. I resolved to sit as still as possible until someone noticed me. And even if they didn't, I wouldn't move, not even for lunch.

The wing chair across from the fireplace was my dad's favorite place to sit. As I pressed my head back into its squishy headrest, I could almost smell his cigarettes. The clove kind like Easter ham baking. I put both my hands on the armrests and gripped them for balance. I was going to remain as still as possible. A piece of furniture or a painting. Frozen until someone remembered to look for me.

Cars pulled up outside and people, giggling and

laughing, with the slaps of meaty hands on backs, strolled from the street to the backyard. The window behind the chair was open, and the people were only a few feet away from me. Not that they even knew. Someone upstairs must have heard the cars because the lock on the bedroom door finally popped and opened. More people walked by outside, laughing even louder. I strained to see past the sides of the chair and out the window. I thought I could hear Louis whooping it up the loudest. "Me, a family guy. Ha! Real funny, Harry, real funny."

Yeah, I thought, real funny. When I turned face-front again to resume my zombie pose, Kate was wiggling her hips in a hurry out of the living room. "Harry!" she screeched not more than three feet behind me.

"What's the deal, baby?" Louis asked. "We've almost got a full house. She coming or what?"

"Yeah, Louis, she's coming, wait 'til ya get a load of her new do," Kate said in her regular ill-tempered way. "Harry, you feel like getting hitched yet?" she cooed.

"You're shameless, Kate, go get my girl down here," Louis barked.

I heard Kate's sigh of exasperation and the folds of her dress as she wiggled, more slowly this time, like a kid, back into the house. She walked through the front door, which she had left open, and paused as if she expected to be greeted. I didn't move.

She strolled over to the fireplace and picked at her

teeth in the mirror above the mantel. She had teeth like a horse, and the lipstick made it worse. Then, she stopped, mouth still open with her eyes on the picture of my parents and me. She picked the frame up in both hands and studied our faces carefully. "Humph," she said, setting the picture on the bookshelf next to the fireplace like a book with only the side of the frame showing.

I wanted to scream what are you doing? but I didn't want to move and break my rule. Just then my mother appeared at the top of the stairs with Marlene behind her. She was in her wedding dress. A straight, off-white satin skirt that skimmed the top of her shoes with a large slit right up to her thigh and a matching lace jacket with gold buttons. I looked at her face, to catch her eye, to get her to notice me so I could move and scream at Kate for touching my family. I stared so hard at my mother's eyes that I almost missed it—her hair, her beautiful red hair, the hair that she got her name from, was gone—dyed the color of Barbie's flowing locks and cut to her chin in a bob. She looked so different from the neck up that she could be someone else's mother entirely.

Before she noticed me, or at least said anything to me, Kate whistled and pointed to where she moved my family to. "Okay?" she whispered to my mom, the woman with the white-blond hair.

Ruby drew her breath in a sort of "oh," but she didn't

yell or scream or even say put it back. She nodded. "Yeah, right. I forgot."

Forgot, I thought, forgot about me, and just as I said that to myself, Marlene extended a blood-red fingernail in my direction.

"The kid gonna take pictures or what?"

"Oh, Hannah, there you are," Ruby said, no good morning, no how are you, no did you eat.

"Here's the camera," Kate said, dropping it into my lap. "It's all set, just hit the button and shoot."

The three of them arranged themselves on the stairs, and I didn't even get up. I aimed the camera at them and hit the button Kate said to. The flash cube popped and exploded in light. In that moment of white light, the entire scene in front of me disappeared. I didn't have to see Ruby with that blond hair or the smiling faces of the others. In that flash, it was gone, they were gone, and I was safely alone.

Monday, October 20, 1997

I wake up at four-thirty in the morning, and the yellow chiffon dress hangs in the open closet in front of the bed like some kind of apparition. My body aches, hungover or quite possibly beaten. The image of my apartment, my own bed, my darkroom, and the unfinished photos of apples flash before me, and I must go back.

I squish my feet into my shoes, grab the dress, and slip past Ruby's door. She rolls over twice and sighs. Allen's sons watch me creep by from inside their walnut and cherry frames. Their happy boyhood faces mimic me, and I try to imagine them sneaking out of the house, holding their breath until they reached the last step. I check an impulse to stick my tongue out at the last boy, Allen's youngest, whose name I can't remember or never knew. The thick carpet muffles footfalls, and the house remains as still as ever. I lower the lid to the secretary by the front door, looking for a piece of paper.

I scrawl *Need to work. Thanks.* on the back of the electric bill and leave the house. In the early morning, the quiet of the streets is even greater than at night, despite the surprisingly eager stream of commuters that parades along the sidewalk in front of Ruby's house. A man in a trench coat carries a maroon briefcase that appears to be a little too heavy for him; a younger guy dressed in khakis with boat shoes follows him with a skateboard under one arm and a beaten L.L. Bean backpack over the other; and a woman, my own age, pounds her navy pumps into the sidewalk as she struts by. Her silky-gray trench coat flutters soundlessly behind her like wings. They create a slight breeze as they pass, like I'm not even standing there, like they can't see me. An older man, in a black wool dress coat, a little slower than the rest, falls into a fairly even pace in front of me. With the black expanse of his coat and his shorter height, he reminds me of a windup penguin.

"When's the next train?" I shout to him.

"The big one leaves at five-forty. About an hour." He picks up his pace a little more and disappears onto the campus. I stop a block before the entrance to the campus, paralyzed with indecision. I collapse against the brown glass doors to an ATM machine alcove. Leaves gather around my feet, and their pointy tips pierce my ankles through my socks. The cast-iron gates of the university loom up above the street, and fog rolls and lumbers through the gates and the spaces between the bars. It reminds me of the entrance to hell in some Greek myth or Dante's *Inferno*. I cannot move.

I do not want to see what is beyond that gate. A forty-something woman with a gray-brown bun and a floral pantsuit charges in front me, her loud footfalls echoing between the walls of the ATM alcove. She slips through the gate, and one of the metal tips of her briefcase catches a cast-iron bar. A clang pulsates through the fog and down the street. I take this as a warning sign and shuffle my feet to free them from the piercing leaves. The air is too cold, and a few other businesspeople turn their heads to look at me when they hear the raspy sound of my breath. I feel myself being watched, so I quickly turn, ever hoping that the last twenty days could have been one huge sick joke.

Behind me a new wave of men—investment professionals, computer consultants, and lawyers of all sorts—rounds the corner onto Nassau. In their navy and blue-black suits and their off-to-work hustle, any one of them could have been Drew. I think about the train ride back to Hoboken, and the entire train filled with people who only look like someone I know. I press myself into the alcove again, unable to watch the captains of industry walk by. I hate to think that I will remember Drew in a suit, being that it had so little to do with how he really used to and still wanted to live.

He used to be a bicycle mechanic with greasy fingers and torn jean shorts. His hair, permanently slicked into place as a stockbroker, stood frizzy from the humidity in Sal's Cycles of Fort Lee. He could put a bike together or take one apart in under ten minutes. Sal used to say admiringly that bicycles were Drew's gift. His parents, on the other hand, used to call it his job playing with toys, and signed him up, without asking permission, to the most expensive Series 7 training classes in all of Manhattan. Dutiful and full of respect for their wishes, he went riding his bicycle across the George Washington Bridge every day in a suit and tie to become the best stockbroker hired by Wallace, Dibgy, and Stern in the last twelve years.

Then we moved to Hoboken, the bicycle went into storage, and he became everything he never was or wanted to be. On the train, surrounded by Coach briefcases, *Wall Street Journals* folded in thirds, and silk ties with understated patterns, I would be lost, swimming in the sea that once surrounded and ultimately drowned Drew. I have no desire to swim today and look up at the cab stand a half a block away from the entrance to the university. Four taxis wait, their headlights piercing the fog, burning it off bit by bit.

The taxis of the town wait for people getting off the

New Jersey Transit bus or emerging from the campus. Not looking like either, I decide this might be a problem, until I realize the dress bag would make me look important, like some debutante or wayward bridesmaid finally sober enough to get home. I decide to stick with that story, and force a deep breath into my lungs and start up the street. I am just some party girl who missed the train back to Hoboken, I tell myself as if I was ever that sort of girl, as if I could even think of partying at this point, as if I will ever be able to do so much as laugh again. The breeze shifts and stings my face; two slight tears squeak out on either side of my eyes. It is the closest I have come to crying in the last twenty days, and I wipe them both away before approaching the first cab.

I tap the passenger window on a newer-model Chevrolet, the kind of car that is oval-shaped and policemen drive, and the taxi driver, without question, unlocks all four doors.

"Where to?" he asks, not even turning around to look at me struggling to put the dress on the hanger hook.

The car smells like after-dinner mints and Old Spice. The electronic fare counter and radio face give off a weird green glow on the blue velour interior. This is not the kind of cab I was used to. "Hoboken," I say, pausing for his response of "Oh, no, I don't go that far." I put my hand on the door, waiting to be asked to get out. But instead of questioning my destination, he puts the cab into gear and pulls out onto the deserted street without even looking in his rearview mirror.

"You do go to Hoboken, the Hoboken by New York, right?" I ask, glancing uneasily over my shoulder as the shops and restaurants of Nassau Street turn into large suburban houses.

"Yeah," he says, "I'll be going north a little to catch the Turnpike at eighteen. Okay with you?"

"Yeah," I say, "okay with me."

He turns up the radio a little. I can barely make it out, but I know from the static that it is one of those AM radio self-help programs. He laughs a few times, slapping his hand on his knee, and I hope the on-air therapist said something funny and that he isn't laughing at the callers.

"What's so funny?" I ask, leaning forward.

He turns the radio up more. "These people," he says, "they make up problems out of thin air. This lady, she thinks her dog talks to her, but she can't understand barking. If only."

"If only what?" I ask. Maybe the dog barks a lot. Maybe this is a big problem like the neighbors are complaining, threatening the dog pound.

"If only that was my biggest problem," he says.

An argumentative feeling wells up inside me, and I want to defend the lady with the dog. I put my better judgment aside as we swing onto the Turnpike. He grabs the ticket from the attendant without stopping and heads toward the Cars-Trucks-Buses lane. "What is your biggest problem?" I ask.

"This is not something a girl your age should want to hear when she should be sleeping off whatever put her in this cab," he says, switching the radio to an oldies station.

He doesn't want to talk to me, but I don't care. The lady with the dog deserves some respect. Everyone with a problem deserves some respect. "This isn't something I can sleep off."

"That's what you people get for taking those chemical things. You should know better by now." He whips the cab around a semi with its hazard lights on.

"No, my fiancé died last month. We were supposed to get married Saturday. Would you mind telling me how I could know better?"

"Listen, I'm sorry. Definitely a problem to work out there. Maybe you could call the Night Doctor."

"Why, so you could laugh at me the whole way back in the cab? Would that be part of your tip? You could go back and tell everyone about the lady with the dog and the woman who wants to marry the dead guy."

"You want to marry the dead guy?" he asks.

"Yes," I say, raising my voice.

"Lemme get you straight. Marry him? Some kind of New Age thing?"

"No, the traditional thing. Dress, cake, flowers on all the tables, open bar," I say, and as I do, the whole reception takes shape in my mind for the first time. I start to see the seating chart and the tasteful music the DJ could play. "Already paid for," I add, taking the opportunity to try out a sample argument on someone not invited or involved.

"They used to do that," he says, "in France, after wars. To make all the little children legitimate. You got kids?"

"No."

"Too bad. Coulda been a legal thing."

I sink back into the seat. The one person who understands me is callous and insensitive to people with problems. I close my eyes, trying to ignore the signs passing by.

"You okay back there? My name is Paulie, by the way. You know, just because I laughed don't mean I don't get it. Listen, let me tell you my problem and you could laugh at that. Okay?"

I don't say anything. I want this ride to be over. I don't want to think about making children legitimate. I want to tell him to turn off at Newark Airport and put myself on a flight to someplace warm, someplace where they don't speak any English.

"You see, I drive this cab all day. Okay job, right? Air-conditioning, see things, meet people, stop for lunch whenever. But this isn't what I like to do. I'm really a painter. Not like Michelangelo or any of that museum stuff. But houses, you know, inside and out. My father was a painter, too. But I can't do it no more. My back broke. Really broke, fell off a ladder. So I can walk and talk and drive this cab, but I can't stand straight enough to get back up a ladder. Mind if I stop for coffee? I could really use some coffee."

I shake my head no and watch as he signals into the Garfield rest area. The car parking lot is mainly empty, but enough tractor trailers line the sides of the road to keep the place more than busy. The trucks idle patiently, their running-board lights all on, waiting for the truckers to wake up or come back from getting breakfast. A German shepherd sits in the driver's seat of a huge blue truck with Alabama plates. I can't help but laugh at the idea of some dog driving a big rig from Alabama to New Jersey.

Paulie pops open the passenger door, startling me from my laughter. He hands me a bag with a coffee in it.

"Sugar and cream in the bottom. See, I told you to laugh at me. Glad you did."

"No, no, the dog, the one driving the truck."

Paulie leans his head out the window. "That is funny," he says. "But I thought it wasn't okay to laugh about dogs."

I smile and begin fixing my coffee. "Thanks," I say, trying to pop the drinking section off the lid.

"You know what I miss most about the painting. The pay was good, and the houses usually nice, but I miss the feeling I got when every inch of the wall was clean and painted. I was done. I could put my buckets and rollers away and be done. Go home, eat, sleep, hold my wife. That is after I showered, you know. She hated the way paint stuck to my arms." He laughs a little more to himself and turns off at 14C.

"You can drop me by the Path Station. That's close enough."

Paulie pays the toll and charges off toward the Holland Tunnel. The bumps in the road feel familiar to me from before our car died on the Long Island Expressway coming back from Jones Beach a few years ago. We went to one of those Earth Day festivals, so we were feeling a little eco-conscious and didn't replace the damn thing. At that moment, I miss having a car, the power to get from point A to point B without having to find someone or something to take you there.

"I will not drop you by the Path Station. I'll drop you at your building. It's five o'clock in the morning, and you never can tell what has been hanging out since the night before."

"But I do live right across from the Path Station. Above the pizza parlor. What do you think, just because I'm grieving I have a death wish? Really, Paulie, I'm smarter than that."

"Really, Paulie," he mimics. "What's your name?"

"Hannah."

"Well, Hannah, here's your stop. Good luck with the wedding."

I hand him a fifty-dollar bill and start to turn away.

"Wedding present," he says, handing it back to me.

I step back from the car to look at him, and as I do, he pulls away from the curb waving. Stupidly, I wave back as the car heads up the street and turns. I try to remember the name of the cab company, but can't. Paulie is going to be one of those mystery things in life that you tell people about late at night, after the dinner dishes have been put away and too much wine has been consumed. A smile warms my face as I push the key into the front door of my building, grateful to finally be home.

I walk into the front door, expecting to find someone, not necessarily Drew, but maybe Rena or Fox-Boy, or possibly a cat. A cat would be nice to come home to. A large orange tiger stripe with a loud meow. Another living being to fill the space, which used to be too small for two. Instead of finding a person or an animal, I find my answering machine with two messages from Miranda, one from someone I don't ever remember meeting, and one from Fox-Boy. Ignoring them, I head for my darkroom and the unattractive piles of apples.

The chemicals are all out of place, rolls of negatives toppled in untidy pyramids all over my workbench. I look over the proofs of the actual, organic product, straining my eyes to see which ones could be reasonably touched up to delete the marks and unappealing colors. I scan through rolls of other takes, deciding on two out of close to one hundred pictures I have taken over the last two months. They would clean up better if they started out bigger, so I pull the original in hopes I could develop a bigger print. But I can't focus long enough on the disorganized rack of chemicals or the timer.

A stack of pictures lies unsorted next to a mess of chemical bottles. Leafing through them, I discover they aren't apple shots. Instead I find him. I close my eyes for a minute and take a deep breath; it is hard to keep finding him—in stacks of photos, in the faces of strangers, the places he should be. I open my eyes slowly to discover a picture of him asleep on Miami Beach. You could see the pink line of his sunburn beginning to form across his back. In the next picture he is leaping up from the lawn chair to stop me from taking any more pictures. *You're on vacation,* he chanted to me as he took my camera away. *Relax,* he said, *be like me.*

His voice comes at me through the walls. I want to open the door to see him standing there, tie undone, his brown hair bushy and pushed back off his forehead. Almost every day he would be waiting for me on the other side of that door, listening to my timer, knowing that after it sounded I would open the door for a few minutes before beginning the next round. It was like he was lonely for my company. Despite all of the people in his world, Drew wanted me. Stupidly, I was always on the other side of that door, completely unable to see that he really truly did want me and that was a fact that couldn't ever be changed—whether I admitted that I wanted him from the top of the Empire State Building to if I actually married him in front of all of our family and friends. I should've trusted the fact that I always felt him on the other side of that door. Instead of being haunted by that feeling now.

I pace around the living room surrounded by images of him. He was my number one subject and would pose no matter what the conditions. My favorite picture is probably the most classic in setting. It was taken the day Drew passed the Series 7 exam, fulfilling his parent's life-long capitalist dream to become a stockbroker. The classic Brooks Brothers shot. Clean, white-toothed smile, navy-blue suit, and an almost flashy tie. To say suit, though, would be wrong; we lost his trousers about three minutes after he got back to the apartment. The picture was an afterthought, and he always liked to remind me that his smile had nothing to do with the test.

The funniest is the Christmas picture from our last year. We spray-painted ourselves green with body paint and hung Christmas ornaments, glass balls and candy canes, from our ears and hair and underclothes, which Drew dyed green in a Laundromat washing machine.

We posed out in the snow behind the apartment building early on Christmas morning when everyone would
still be asleep or under their own trees, and would take
no notice of two crazy people like us dressed as trees. It
was so cold in the snow, but he held me tightly, the
warmth of his body swallowing me like a down blanket.

I stop near his desk and lift up the top layers of papers;
it is mainly wedding stuff, lists of people to invite,
already-paid bills to the Manor, and lists of dates and
times for airlines without destinations. I decide then to
start with the guest list. Beginning with distant relatives
and friends, I work my way in.

"The wedding is still on," I say, rushing through it,
hoping that if I say it fast enough the picture would be in
focus. Hoping that Aunt Katie would go, oh, okay, two
o'clock next Saturday. Hoping the Morgansterns would
congratulate me on my good sense in going through
with it. But hoping isn't enough.

"Who is this?" ask Mr. Morganstern, Aunt Sally, and
Drew's boss.

"Why ever on earth would you do something as
insane as that? Like who would want to marry you later.
Think about it," yells my cousin, who lives in Teaneck,
over the din of her four children all under the age of
five. "But hey, free food?"

Mrs. Livinia, the stoop-lady from downstairs, offers a
good shrink. "He has sliding scale and everything. Go

and let it out private," she tells me reassuringly. "You'll feel better."

By the fifth call, I stop dialing and decide on some answers. There are things to be considered, feelings of relatives and my own desire that everyone actually show up. I think about explaining the whole situation. My foot-dragging, my refusal to wear the heirloom engagement ring for fear of theft, the fighting with Drew about the bath mat, but they wouldn't get it. I could say it is part of my religion, some sort of New Age tradition, but both our families know I am just as much of a lapsed Protestant as everyone else. I could say it is a healing ritual or that a psychic told me to do it. Or put it in terms everyone can understand: It was already paid for. After all, it worked with Paulie the Cab Driver, and Ruby didn't protest. And it wouldn't even be a lie; Drew made sure it was paid for, not wanting my mother's fourth husband, a man we both met only twice, to feel obligated.

"It's already paid for," I say to Drew's sister's answering machine. "Drew never appreciated waste," I add, slightly surprised that I'm not lying about this, although it was more true with bicycle parts than it was with money. To Drew, money was something to play with, and that's what made him the best broker in his firm. Bicycle parts could be amassed and turned into more bicycles. I chuckle a little under my breath at the thought process, hoping the machine won't pick it up as background noise.

Aunt Josephine, sister to Sally, agrees almost instantly. As do the three men who share a desk with Drew at the firm, some of his aunts I don't believe I've ever met, and my other cousin, Vincent of Paramus. A few of the older ladies, friends of my mother and Mrs. Heinz, pause with horrified gasps. "I never really got a chance to talk with everyone at the funeral, it would be a great chance to remember him, and say good-bye," I fill in quickly, finding the most socially acceptable reason I can think of for those women of society. But my elation at making it through three quarters of the list soon fades as the calls circle around his parents and my friends.

Trying my friends first, I get lucky when both Rena and Fox-Boy are at home together in Rena's apartment, trying to give each other facials. "Oh, honey," Rena says, "come on over, we'll get rid of those tearstains in a jiffy. No more crying for a pretty girl like you."

"No, Rena, no facial for me today, and I'm surprised that Fox-Boy is letting you. People might question his, you know."

"Like they don't already," Fox-Boy shouts from behind Rena. Fox-Boy is the victim of being every woman's best friend and the one people wink about at parties and men avoid in locker rooms.

"Do you need something, sweetie? Can we help?"

"I want you to come to my wedding," I say quickly,

wanting to get it all out in the open before talk returns to facials.

"Of course you did, that would be why you sent out invitations, now isn't it." The timer goes off in the background, and Fox-Boy starts yelling, "Rena, you got to take it off now or it'll get hard. Immediately. It says right here."

"Relax," she says. "Now, I really appreciate this sentiment. Are you sure you're okay?"

"You're not getting my point. I'm still having the wedding. A sort of celebration. And I still want you and Fox-Boy to come."

"She's having it anyway," Rena whispers.

"What, she isn't pregnant, is she?" Fox-Boy whispers back but so obviously close to the phone that I can hear every word and inflection.

"No, Fox-Boy, I'm having the wedding. Not a baby," I say loudly, knowing his face is pressed against Rena's cheek, listening to every word now that a scandal might be involved.

"Parfait!" Fox-Boy says. "I'll go get my tuxedo. Everyone could use something like a party after this. Tell her I think it's a great idea."

"Did you hear him?" Rena asks.

"Yes, but I didn't hear you. Rena, you okay with this? You'll be there?"

There is a long pause. Then the sound of tap water and a teapot filling up. I step into the kitchen and fill my own teapot. The plants in the windowsill are dying. I pull them one by one into the kitchen sink to pick off the dead parts, leaving more plant in the sink than in the pot.

"Drew used to take care of the plants," I say.

"Yeah," Rena says.

"You'll come?"

"Fix them up then, you know how," she says, quiet and serious. "Come on, you're so capable. You keep everything together." Her voice fades away from the phone like a transatlantic call. I can almost see the far-off look she gets when she's thinking about something.

"But you'll come, right?"

"Before I answer, tell me what is this nonsense really about?"

"Nonsense," I say quietly. "Screw off." Dirt fills in the jagged half-moons of my fingernails, but it feels good and cool. I return the plants to the windowsill and open the blinds. A sunbeam hits the floor, reminding me of when the hospital called. I listen for the microwave, but it doesn't make a sound.

"Please, this can't be serious—it isn't healthy."

"Rena, are you coming or not?" I slide my foot tentatively into the sunny spot on the floor.

"Hannah, he isn't coming back."

And I wish no one would say that to me. Dead meant

never coming back. Gone. Decomposing. I knew that. "If you're not going to understand, I can't explain it to you."

I turn off the phone and pace around the kitchen trying to get up enough nerve to call his parents. We don't exactly have a phone relationship, and I could tell that they blame me for this, for him living away from them, for him being with me, for him dying. I know this, even understand it, but it doesn't make calling them any easier.

I dial their number, which Drew had carefully printed on the important phone numbers list right between the Thai food take-out and the pizza delivery place. I let it ring twice before hanging up. In my mind, the justification for going through with this wedding makes perfect sense. This is my way of shouting from the highest mountain that I meant it when I told him that I would marry him, that I wasn't lying and biding my time waiting for something else. To Mr. and Mrs. Heinz, this will be treason of the highest degree. I hit redial on the phone, cutting it off before the first ring, opting instead to do something civil, something like a tasteful note.

First I write: *Mr. and Mrs. Heinz, I just wanted to take a moment to thank you for Drew, and to let you know that because of my great love for him, I am planning to continue with the wedding as listed in the invitation.*

Then after setting the first aside, I write: *Eleanor and*

Frederick, Just a note to let you know we will be having the wedding as previously scheduled. Thanks, Hannah.

I cross out the *we* and replace it with *I*, then rip up both notes. Four sheets of paper are left from the stationery set they gave me last Christmas, and I am bound and determined to get this over. *Mr. and Mrs. Heinz,* I begin, *please accept my sincerest regrets over the passing of Drew. You both may not have been aware how deeply and truly I cared about your son and looked forward to our life together. This loss effects us all. Please understand that what I am about to tell you is not to hurt or harm anyone but to heal. I am going through with the wedding as Drew planned. I would like to say I planned this wedding right alongside him, but I didn't. I want to make up for this fact in front of everyone Drew and I loved, and hopefully in some way, Drew himself. Thank you for raising Drew up to be the man I knew. Please accept this only with respect. Regards, Hannah*

I place the note in an envelope, seal it, stamp it, and carefully carry it down to the mailbox on the street. I think about Mr. and Mrs. Heinz and whether or not they deserve this. On the street in front of the mailbox, I stare at the envelope, turning it around in my hands to get the feel of it. To assess its weight. Its impact. And a part of me doesn't care if they deserve it or not; it isn't about them or anyone else.

A mail truck pulls alongside the curb, and the mailman begins emptying the box. "You mailing that," he says.

"Yeah," I say, handing it to him.

He gets back into his truck, and I watch him pull away and head up the street. The whole thing is out of my hands. I am going to get this wedding together despite Mr. and Mrs. Heinz, Rena, or myself. This attitude puts a lightness in my heart, until I turn instinctively to look for Drew. I almost feel him standing next to me in that empty space of sidewalk, and it is a feeling I never want to give up as I start up the street, no particular destination in mind.

There are so many people in this world. So many people in this city. They brush past me, bumping into my bag. I feel taller and out of place on the street, with the old-timer women of the neighborhood. These ladies shuffle around me into stores and apartment buildings. I'm not that tall, though. I stop in front of the bakery. I can't be more than five seven. Drew was six foot two and proud of it. When I wore heels, lifting myself up into his range, he would throw his shoulders back like a rooster and swivel his head around.

"Just take a look at it," he said, "do you see how beautiful it is up here, a really different perspective, huh?"

I'd nod and totter off in search of the purse to match

the shoes, especially envious of how much he liked himself and the world in which he lived.

My reflection disappears as people enter the store through the door, little bells announcing their arrival. They stand in front of the counter, smile at the woman in the white half apron that holds back a voluptuous roll of fat, and then point to the confections in the lighted case. The woman behind the counter places the confections in a waxed white box before placing it half on the counter and half off. The woman, possibly the very Mrs. Inganmorte that the letters on the window spell out, quickly winds yards of red string around the box, finishing it off in a little knot at the top of the box. The door opens again, and the smell of bread escapes out into the street. The smell of baked goods always comforts me. Not because I like to eat them, but because that smell comes with warmth. A deep penetrating warmth.

I pull open the door, and I am surprised when the bells ring for me as they did for everyone else. I walk the length of the counter a few minutes, noticing that the name tag of the woman behind the counter reads MRS. INGANMORTE in pink letters. Purim cookies with poppy, prune, and apricot filling rest in triangular piles on top of the counter. Cupcakes, both chocolate and vanilla, are topped with orange frosting and plastic witches in anticipation of Halloween. A paper-doll chain of fall leaves droops down and back up along the baskets of challah, baguettes, and rye breads. The woman smiles and nods at me. I smile and nod back.

Slowly, I ease myself over to the book that rests on the top end of the counter, all the way to the far left side. Inside, there are pictures that put any gourmet magazine to shame. Martha Stewart's creations pale in comparison to Inganmorte's. Mrs. Inganmorte watches me for a few minutes from the doorway to the kitchen, before coming over. I pause at a few different pages before settling on an all-white three-tiered cake with fresh white peonies and lilies garnishing the top and base. I point to the picture and slide my credit card over into Mrs. Inganmorte's floury fingers.

"Saturday," I whisper. "At the Manor."

My mind focuses on the image of her flour-dusted cuticles as I cross the street to my building, and I remember I am hungry. But I suppose this is what Ruby is so worried about, that I will forget things like eating. Baking something, something sweet and heavy, comes to mind. The soft feel of flour under my own manicured nails, the good smells, and the warm oven.

But I haven't ever baked. There never seemed a reason to until now. Running up the stairs and into my apartment, I make a dash for the bookshelf and the cookie cookbook Drew's sister, Miranda, gave me for Christmas last year. Every picture looks good. Powdered sugar, little sculpted shapes, reindeers with red noses, tarts filled with raspberries, lacy cookies made of drizzled chocolate. I search through the recipes for something familiar and easy like sugar cookies.

I start with a bowl and the all-purpose measuring cup. Shockingly enough, we own all six ingredients: baking soda, sugar, vanilla, flour, butter, and eggs. If a stranger asked me to borrow any one of those items, I would shake my head no and say, "We don't keep those in the house." Imagine not knowing what is in your own kitchen. Imagine not knowing.

"Imagine knowing," I say out loud to myself as I add some extra vanilla. I open up the spice cabinet over the range and pull down a few more canisters, unscrewing the lid off of each. I add some cinnamon. Some pumpkin-pie spice. Some cream of tarter. Red sugar sprinkles. Rainbow jimmies. And then I stir, whipping the batter into a bumpy rainbow of sugar, spice, and butter. Absentmindedly, I lick the spoon. The batter is the first thing to go smoothly down in what feels like years. I plunge my fingers down into the greasy paste, letting the dough cling to the pads of my fingers and the crevices of my cuticles. I take all of my fingers into my mouth, but do so quickly, not caring to get all of the batter off before scraping the bowl for more.

I take the bowl from the kitchen and sit down in front of the television. I flip through the channels looking for human voices. The message light on my answering machine blinks rapidly on the table next to me, but those are not the voices I want to hear. Excited and happy people, not always happy, but mainly so, used to walk through these rooms and call me on the phone. I want to hear people who aren't sorry or worried or even the slightest bit concerned. First, I try a game show, but the contestants turn down their glib smiles after a few losing questions. I surf through the channels until I get to the Home Shopping Club. A woman with painted fingernails is pushing a vacuum that is supposed to suck everything up without releasing the slightest molecule back into the air. I stop there. Another woman, the host of the show, starts taking callers.

"Here's a toot for you," she screams, squeezing an old-fashioned bicycle horn to the delight of the caller. I clap my dough-covered hands together to encourage her.

"You called on the testimonial line, do you have a testimonial for us about this wonderful hepa-filtered vacuum?" Diane, the host, asks.

"Of course I do, Diane," answers Phyllis from Ben Salem before launching into a glorious description of her allergen-free home. "The dust is just gone, gone, gone," Phyllis says with such enthusiasm that if I had carpeting I would buy one.

"This really could clean up any mess," Diane repeats over and over again, the picture of the woman with the vacuum never fading from the screen, the ticker of all the orders placed rising at a rate of three per minute. "Look at all those people out there," Diane says, "people just like you." Then the music picks up in the background, and Diane perks up a bit. Honking her horn a few times out of rhythm with the calliope music pouring into the set, Diane announces the hour we've all been waiting for. "It's time" honk "to enter" honk honk "the Diamondze Zone." They pan to the woman with the vacuum clapping wildly at the thought of the Diamondze Zone, or perhaps because she gets to stop vacuuming that three-foot piece of carpet.

Balancing a bit of dough on each of my five right-hand fingers, I sit in awe of the cavalcade of fake diamond creations that blink on and off my screen as Diane gives us the complete tour of the hour ahead. If only I would have known how cheap a fake diamond was when Drew gave me his grandmother's heirloom engagement ring. I could have bought a fake and worn that, so that when people oohed and aahed over our engagement and grabbed rudely for my hand, they would have found something. When they found my fingers empty, free of the glitter that a two-carat heirloom ring can bring, the whispers began.

Even Drew was inclined to side with them. So when I tried to explain my fears of having it stolen while taking pictures in Pelham Bay Park or even Central Park, everyone including Drew looked at me with wide eyes and said, *Well then, stop, stop taking pictures in dangerous places.* Even though the collection I was commissioned to finish by the 3rd Street Gallery was titled *Dangerous Places,* and my last photo to win a prize was of homeless men peeing into the Hudson River, looking back at me like I was crazy for not thinking of that myself.

And the only thing I thought I was crazy for was not telling Drew that I felt abandoned when he said stop. I felt like marriage meant having to give up important things like my work or our friendship, which was based on respect. I should have stopped and said something right then and there instead of letting it build up, and out of my hands, until I was dragging my feet about the type of icing I wanted on a cake and what color boutonniere he should wear to the rehearsal dinner.

"But wait," Diane calls out over the pictures of Diamondzes. "We have one more vacuum to go before we can let those beautiful Diamondzes fly out of here. She begins the list of features quickly and breathlessly: "Allergen removal, dust containment, filtered in- and outflow, quiet and cool-running 6.6 horsepower engine . . . " The picture shifts awkwardly back to the woman with painted fingernails. A stagehand backs away from her as she slips rings on her fingers from a black velvet case. Another stagehand appears from behind thrusting the last vacuum cleaner at her. The woman with the painted fingernails struggles to smile and push the upright on the small corner of rug in front of her. The camera remains wide, not wanting to settle in too close to the struggling spokesmodel.

I look down at my bowl, mostly empty, and my sticky fingers. I think about all the little pieces of Drew around the apartment, those little pieces that would be called allergens and dust, and I'm not sold. I don't think even the world's strongest vacuum could help me clean up and sort through what was okay and what was now considered a mess.

The camera angle tightens on the spokesmodel. Order now, she mouths to the audience before the camera trails down to the shank of the vacuum and to the Diamondze rings on each of her ten fingers. Order now.

"Last minute, folks," Diane chimes in over the glittering image of the spokesmodel and her manicured and many-ringed fingers.

And I feel myself falling to sleep, the half-eaten bowl of sugar-cookie batter sliding off and onto the floor. I watch it go, and the bowl, rocking back and forth, doesn't tip.

Wednesday, April 15, 1992

We giggle a little as the innkeeper asks us in a hush tone if we could pay for the rest of our stay in advance. "We're trying to pay the taxes," she says, pointing at the calendar on the wall behind her, the fifteenth circled in bright red pen. We giggle because our trip was funded by our tax returns, which Miranda miraculously prepared for us, months ago, as part of some accounting course her parents forced her into.

"Sure," I say, handing the innkeeper another crisp one-hundred-dollar bill over Rena's back as she sorts through her fanny pack for hers.

"And the gentleman?" the innkeeper asks.

Rena and I look at each other. The gentleman? Miranda's brother, Drew, was set to arrive sometime this afternoon and take us on—and I quote—"the ride of our life" on mountain bikes. I guess neither one of us realized he would be staying the night as well. But it only makes sense, his return was also done by Miranda. Rena scrunches her eyebrows at me, so I shrug back at her. I pull out a fifty-dollar bill. "Split it?" I ask Rena.

"Yeah, I sure hope he's worth it," she says.

We hadn't met Miranda's brother prior to this trip for the very reason he was coming along. The mountain-bike business kept him occupied 365 days a year. He apparently had some special talent that kept him employed in Fort Lee and, during the winter, around the country leading trips and doing demos for companies. Miranda frequently sported T-shirts from the many places her brother worked.

The innkeeper's husband nods gratefully to us as he clears the few scraps that remained of our cream cheese and marmalade-filled biscuits and our empty coffee cups. "So," I say to Rena as she rapidly flips through the tourism guide set up by the bed-and-breakfast, "what do we do until the gentleman arrives for our bicycle tour?"

"If you think I'm going mountain biking, you are out of your mind. I'm going shopping. This is Taos, H. More artwork and jewelry than anyplace except Santa Fe, and I might drive down there this afternoon." She grins proudly as she points to the brochure titled Shopping Wonderland. I can almost see the gleam of her credit card's hologram in her eye.

"But—"

"But what? I only told Miranda I would think about it, and she didn't even come, so I don't see how I should be kept from shopping to do something athletic."

"You sound like my mother," I say, getting up from the table and heading for the door to the back porch. "I'll stay here and wait for the gentleman."

"Isn't that more like your mother?" Rena calls out sharply, wounding me somewhere in the side as if she poked me with a sharpened stick.

I look at her for a minute pouring over the brochures in the album on the table. She didn't even look up to say it. It was only a joke. But it hurt, and to explain that would be to admit that what my mother did bothered me. And in order to be bothered, one had to first care. If she wants to date and marry every man she meets, so be it. I shake my head and step out onto the deck.

Miranda should be given credit for finding such a great place to stay. From the deck off of the back of the adobe main house you can see over the adobe wall and past the dry flat land dotted with pine-nut trees that separates Taos from the mountains. Shadows of clouds cast themselves on the tree-lined and snow-touched mountains. Their dark shapes move silently over the tops of the trees in the distance. Only a cloud could move so rapidly and not change anything it cast its shadow on. I stand in envy of the mountain, the trees, the snow that won't melt, and the clean that surrounds it all. It has been this way for thousands of years, and it will stay that way for thousands more.

I walk back to our room. Rena's walking shoes are gone, and so is she. I peak through the lace curtains and find that so is the rental car from the parking lot. A pink piece of paper sits folded like a tent on the shelf around the kiva fireplace. *H—If I'm not back tonight, don't worry. I might spend the night in Santa Fe if I can't buy it all in one day—Rena.* I toss the paper into the fireplace and look forward to watching it burn later. How nice of her to leave me without a car and waiting for a man I never met to take me on a death ride through the mountains. Such a friend, I say to myself as I flop backward onto her unmade bed.

The silence of the place fills me. I don't think I have spent a single moment in complete silence since I moved back to New Jersey after college. Even at four in the morning, Jersey City can be wailing with sirens, drunk men on the street, or the couple upstairs being amorous and loud about it. Drawing my breath in deeply, I think Zen thoughts. Beautiful mountain vistas, streams rushing over rocks, cactus with flowers. I remember my camera frantically, the way a mother remembers a child when she realizes that child is no longer right at her side in the department store. I rummage through two of my bags before finding it on the beside table—where I left it after taking a picture of Rena in front of the kiva fireplace and the fire she started last night.

After checking for film, I pull on my hiking boots, which Miranda insisted I buy for the trip, and head out for the flat dry land behind the bed-and-breakfast. When I think desert, I think nothing, but this space of land is more than nothing. There's the golden-orange color of the dusty ground. The pine-nut trees, small, round, evergreen-like bushes that grow like weeds because no one has found a way to efficiently harvest their pine nuts. I like the idea of that—being able to grow free because people haven't found a way to use you yet. I almost think that that is the difference between Ruby and me. My mother likes to be harvested, collected into neat suburban houses, and I like to be free.

There are birds flying above, and little plants of many light shades of green creep along the ground like weeds in sidewalks of Manhattan or Jersey City. The piñon trees shiver in a slight, dry breeze. Little puffs of dust rise up and then fall away, leaving only a cloudy trace on the toe of my boot. This is a place of surprises. Driving into town on the low road, we passed over the Rio Grande, which from a distance runs invisibly through the ground leaving lush green overgrowth in the wake of its steep sides. From a hundred feet away, you couldn't tell why there was a bridge.

I turn around, and the Rio Bed & Breakfast has disappeared. Its high adobe-fence wall merges with the sand and disappears in the shimmer of heat that is beginning as the sun takes its place high in the sky. Through the lens of the camera I can make out the scrollwork of the cast-iron gate. I snap one picture, then point my lens at the sky and snap another. I crouch down on the ground and lower my lens inches above the sand. I snap the sand and then raise the lens a little to shoot the creeping plants at an angle.

I stand up, satisfied, and brush the desert off my knees. The little black mica flakes slip slowly through the air before settling indiscriminately back into the sand. It was the kind of thing I would take pictures of, a small thing, and if I had known how beautiful mica was when drifting back to earth, I would have had my camera ready. The small things make up the big things like one-thousand-piece puzzles.

I remember doing the same puzzles over and over again as a child until my mother's second husband, Louis, brought home a container of puzzle glue for me. After gluing the first one together I was amazed at how from a distance it looked like any other picture Ruby had hanging. Only up close could you see the fault lines and connecting spaces in between the puzzle pieces. After gluing a few of my favorites together and hanging them up in faux father-daughter moments, I regretted their solidity.

The fun was over after you stuck all the pieces together with permanent glue.

I take a few more pictures of the bed-and-breakfast before I see someone waving at me from on top of the adobe wall. The person waves like the people on the runways who park airplanes into specific gates. All that is missing is the orange cones and safety vest. I walk toward the wall and the person and slowly discover that it is a man waving me in. He stops waving as I begin walking in his direction and cups his hands around either side of his mouth. "Hannah," he bellows, "is that you?"

I mimic his motions and bellow back, "Yes." Then I decide it must be only one person. "Drew, is that you?"

When I am within ten feet of the adobe wall, he puts a hand across his forehead like a brave scout. He looks me over from head to toe. "You'll be fine," he says, jumping down in front of me.

"Yes, I will be fine, but what does that have to do with you?"

"I'm Drew," he says.

"Yes," I say, "and how does that make me fine?"

"Many ways, many ways." He extends his dusty palm to me. His eyes move up and down my dust-covered body in a most pleasing fashion.

I lightly accept his handshake. He pulls a tricky one, moving his fingers around mine in a sort of secret handshake people do at bars. I smile and let my hand follow his through the pattern.

"Well, now, you'll be even better than I thought."

"Do you mean the bike ride?" I ask, taking a stab at his enigma.

He put his hands on his hips. "Bingo," he says. "You're not one of Miranda's cooking-school friends that ate a little too much of their homework. I was worried, you know, the mountains can be a hard place to trek."

"Trek?"

"Yeah, I thought we were going for a ride." Drew says over his shoulder as he turns and walks along the wall of the Rio. "The bikes are ready, are you?"

I skip a few steps to catch up with him. "What are you going to do to me if I'm not?"

He doesn't answer, and instead, he turns his head to face me, and smiles the most dazzling smile I have ever seen. The sun sparkles off of his left incisor like a charm or commercial retouch. I knew at that moment that with him I was never going to be ready. I knew that I was always going to be caught off guard, and that for the first time in my life, that might be the best place to be.

Tuesday, October 21, 1997

Morning surprises me on the couch. The still light from the streetlamps peeks into the living room under the shades. I jerk the shades back and send them rolling and snapping to the top. Standing in the false light, hands on my hips, I watch the world moving below. Trucks pull up to the loading docks of the corner grocery and the diner and the bakery and the florist. Men in uniforms load handtrucks, push them into the stores then back out. The trucks pull away, leaving no trace of having been there, and I'm not surprised by this. It seems that no man is meant to leave a trace.

I remember being drunk in college and staying out until four in the morning. The way the streets of New London were silent, and the traffic lights changed without any cars driving by. In the winter, and it was almost always winter, the ice reflected the switching lights in their pattern, moving from green to yellow to red, the flashing orange Don't Walk to the white Walk. It was like the whole place was trying to say something, only to take it back when it realized no one was there to hear it. I stumbled back to my apartment because of the cheap beer and the thin sheet of ice that covered everything, and I would sleep restlessly until four in the afternoon. I long to sleep like that again as I stretch my arms above my head, my shoulders stiff from the couch cushions.

Sleeping, in fact, was what separated Drew from the rest of the men I had known. On the few occasions when I was followed home across the thin sheets of ice on the sidewalks of New London, invariably the man following me provided only disturbance to my sleep, however drunken or needed. Drew was better than a blanket. And since I was a little girl I clung to the belief that a blanket could keep the monsters or ghosts from attacking you in your sleep. With Drew, I could sleep naked on a blanketless bed and be both safe and warm.

The second round of trucks pull up below. One back-fires pulling away from the curb, upsetting a calico cat that lives behind the bakery's Dumpster. I want to scoop the cat up, bring it inside, wash it, and give it something to eat. Give it a home. But it isn't a friendly cat, doesn't even like to have its picture taken, running behind the Dumpster whenever anyone gets too close. Pictures, I think, remembering the apples, their deadline, and that it is after all a weekday, a day when most people, even freelancers, go to work.

My morning routine used to begin the minute Drew walked out of the bedroom and into the kitchen for coffee. I'd jump from bed and into the shower, finishing in under five minutes. Blow-dry my hair and brush my teeth for another five. Being an artist in the corporate world made my daily clothing choice simple. Black blazers, slacks, leggings, sweaters, and skirts hung from every other hanger in my closet. In the absence of color coordination, dressing took mere seconds. I would meet him by the door as he was ready to step out.

Today, I take my time in turning away from the window and rest my palms on the chipping paint, warm from the radiator below. I let the warmth flow into my hands, reminding me of sitting on the radiator in my grandparents' house as I waited for my mother to come back from the Hartford train station and her increasingly longer days at work. I would sit on that radiator, collecting its heat, trying each day to stay longer and longer, trying to stay in that one place until she rounded the corner of the driveway. The minute I spotted her, I would dash from my spot into the kitchen and upstairs to what was being used as my room. Arranging my books and papers around me, I would take my place in the middle of the cold floor, still waiting for her to come and find me. The heat from the radiator, however much I may have thought I stored, was almost never enough to keep me warm until Ruby poked her head in the doorway to say hello.

I pick up the cordless phone from the back of the couch and dial Rena at work. I didn't like leaving things in such a bad way.

"Hello, Mircom Enterprises, Stacey speaking."

"Rena Falconniere, please."

"So sorry," Stacey sings, "she's, like, out today."

"Sick?" I ask.

"Yes, if you call working too late in a go-go bar last night sick." And with that, Stacey leaves me hanging on the phone.

Rena's latest evening exploit was working as a Safety Controller at the Pussy Cat Lounge in Fairfield, Connecticut. It was her job to make sure the girls didn't smoke or shoot up or snort anything backstage before they went on. The Lounge, as regulars call it, got into a little dispute with their insurance agency when a dancer fell off the stage because of some acid-induced vision she was having. Rena's job prevented the insurance company from dropping The Lounge and paid her twenty dollars an hour to watch the girls and stay straight herself. I guess she didn't explain her new job as well to Stacey as she did to me.

I turn the phone on and press my fingers lightly across

Rena's number. I listen to the ring on her side and hope she answers the phone. Fox-Boy answers instead with a "Hello, hello, hello."

"Fox-Boy? It's Hannah, Rena okay?"

"Yeah, sleeping." He doesn't say anything else, leaving me to ask.

"And you're sleeping with her?"

"Ha, not quite, arguing until five in the morning about the stupidity of that new profession she has taken on. In fact, I was just leaving, for work, a real job, in a brightly lit office building where she should be and isn't." He clicks off abruptly.

I hang up the phone and begin to consider going to work myself. In the bedroom, I stand in front of the closet. I could put my hand on the knob and turn three quarters to the right and open the door and step inside. I could step inside and turn on the light and look at my clothes hanging every which way from all types of hangers. I could look at my clothes with my back to where his clothes used to be. Or I could turn around and see the wide empty spaces that used to be his suits, shirts, sports blazers, jeans, sweaters, and ties sitting on shelves or hanging from hooks. He had so much in that closet that when you opened the door the smell of him—his aftershave mingled with laundry soap—would roll out in a gust. Now just a whiff remains, in the carpet or the paint, and each time I open the door it grows less and less. I could open the closet and be surrounded at once by both him and his absence. I step away from the closet and sink down onto the unmade bed.

If things had gone differently, I would be sitting on this very bed trying to pack for a honeymoon. Not that I even knew where it was going to be; Drew's big plan was to surprise me or bribe me depending on how you looked at it. He wouldn't tell me even the slightest detail about our destination—not even if I should pack for hot or cold weather. *Both,* he told me, *that way you'll be prepared no matter what.* It did start out as a surprise for me, but the more I hemmed and hawed about flowers and disc jockeys, the more he used it as a bribe.

Come on, Hannah, he'd say, *pick this and we're one step closer to*—and he'd take a dramatic deep breath—*one step closer to, come on, Hannah, fill in the blank, one step closer to . . . vacation.* And for a while the thought of going somewhere else, for a week, without caterers to call, tuxedos to be ordered, and flowers to coordinate, a week alone, just the two of us, worked on lightening my mood and made the planning easier. Thinking about Drew and the honeymoon, my neck tightens into a knot. My behavior was embarrassing at best. Foolish. Unfortunate. Irreversible. I flop back down on the bed, trying to release the thought with some mind-erasing sleep.

But thoughts of my work dance frantically about me and the calm of sleep slips away. I must get dressed. I must propel my body downtown to the skyscrapers of doom and into the dark room made of steel. I must develop picture after picture until the organic apples look as good as those with alar. I roll over on the bed, still not moving anywhere. The digital clock slips from minute to minute with a slight electronic noise. It is getting old, I think, and so am I.

After heaving myself up, I pull on the lower dresser drawer and find the last resort—black leggings. I pull out a long-sleeved black T-shirt from the drawer above that and head into the shower. Avoiding looking in the mirror, I step into the scalding water willingly, realizing that my hair is as greasy as John Travolta's, and that I may not have showered yesterday. Yesterday. I rub shampoo into my hair and try to imagine what I did yesterday. The cake. The phone calls. Rena.

I soap up the rest of my body quickly, scrubbing hard with the loofah to remove the dead skin cells and rinse off just as quickly. With the oversized purple towel Drew used in his college dorm wrapped around my dripping body, I pad into the kitchen to find the cordless phone, leaving little puddles behind me on the wood floor. I dial Rena and let it ring until the machine is about to pick up. I dial again, letting it ring for just as long. I do this four times before she answers.

"Yes, John," she says, expecting it to be Fox-Boy bothering her, and not me.

"Rena, it's Hannah. I need to talk to you."

"Listen, my head hurts, one of the chicks slipped something into my Sprite for kicks last night. Can I call you later?"

"No."

"No?"

"No, I don't want to let this go on any longer than I have to. Are you coming on Saturday?"

"Of course," Rena answers as if there was no other answer in the world.

"But yesterday—"

"Yes, yesterday. I think you're nuts, but if you want to be nuts, so be it."

"So be it?" I ask, unsure of the ramifications of being nuts.

"So be it. And if you want some help being nuts, just ask. Fox-Boy will tell you, he thinks I'm as crazy as a loon for working at the Pussy."

"You are crazy for working at the Pussy," I tell her.

She laughs a little and groans with pain. "My head." She sighs. "Let me die in peace."

"Fine," I say, "you die, and I'll go to work."

"Not work, anything but work, even wedding planning for God's sake, just not work."

"Someone's got to go," I tell her before hanging up.

I look at the cordless phone for a few seconds and let the idea of being crazy roll around in my head. Am I nuts, I wonder. I set the phone down and grab a glass from the cabinet. Filling it up from the sink, I look at the calendar again and remember how warm Drew was when it was cold outside. As the sun went down in the pumpkin field, the end-of-fall chill blew in and my fingers were freezing. He tucked my hands into his pockets and wrapped his warm fingers around mine. I'm not nuts, I think, just cold and lonely.

The street is as I would expect it to be, and for the first time in my life, I can say I have something to rely on. The streets of Hoboken will always be crowded. This could be some sort of mantra for me, something I could repeat in the dark of my bedroom as I imagine hearing Drew's breathing and strain to hear the impossible. There will be real people on the streets, I could say. Or I could change it to something a little more personal, a little more true. Something like: At least you won't be alone in the morning. Knowing all too well that I will be alone and listening to imagined sounds throughout the night.

The station is on the verge of being crowded with the people who worked in the city and are late. They huddle bleary-eyed on the platform, scanning newspapers in one hand, drinking coffee with the other. They stand on the train in much the same fashion, only they sway with each jerk as if their bodies have the track memorized. I sit away from them, portfolio on my lap, always unsure of their lidless coffee mugs and overconfident, not-holding-on surfer stance. They are people on top of things, and Drew used to fit right in with them, trading sections of the *Wall Street Journal* with fellow suited passengers, meeting them later for express lunches in between trades. I want to warn them. Tell them to slow down, to quit grabbing fatty hot dogs and too much coffee, but they only stare at their papers or straight ahead, not seeing a damn thing.

The train pulls into the World Trade Center, flipping an unseen switch on the comatose riders. They bolt from the train running toward and up the escalators. I hang back, watching them, wishing I could be like them a little, and let the world go by without noticing. I pull myself onto the escalator, letting it propel me to the top without resistance. The first few hazy rays of sunshine make their way through to the street and warm up the smell of decay and exhaust fumes. Thankfully, my office isn't too far away, and somehow, my feet know where to take the rest of me.

I couldn't believe I lived with all of this—Hoboken being not much better than Manhattan. The hordes of people, the air constantly smelly, the threat of theft or bodily harm. I try to keep pace with the crowd around me, but my eyes are drawn to things on the sidewalk: the hot pink flyers from the triple-X clubs that exclaim in bold letters NUDE, NUDE, ALL NUDE, the crushed coffee cups from Greek diners with their portraits of Zeus and Athena wrinkled and stained, and wads of gum marked by the soles of shoes like fingerprints. But it was where we lived; we found the apartment, settled in, got used to public transportation.

After six years, the thought of stopping makes my insides shake as I ride the elevator up to the fourteenth floor. This is the only thing I know how to do. With portfolio in hand, I brace myself for the worst, hoping all the desktop designers and printers' agents, including Miranda, Drew's younger sister, are in a meeting well away from view. It's not that I don't like them; in fact, Miranda was at one time one of my closest friends. But people act startled around me. As if I remind them of some unpleasant fact they would much rather forget. I hate to see the looks of sympathy and unease as I pass by people who used to greet me with smiles and scowls alike. When everything changes, it is hard to know what or who to trust.

The elevator doors slide open, and everyone is in their rightful place in the sea of lavender cubicles, deleting and adding words and pictures to the multitude of marketing pieces that escaped the company's walls on a daily basis. All the cubicles are made of half walls, except for the supervisors, who sit in high Plexiglas alcoves like fish tanks. Miranda has an office in the back corner, your standard window office. I look down at the carpet, hoping to avert seeing anyone or hearing any more words of condolence. My feet thud against the hard industrial-grade carpet. My shoes, black and battered, look out of place against the cool sea-breeze tones of the flooring. I slip quickly into the first darkroom, turn out the lights to avoiding seeing more than I have to, and start on processing the prints to the size I need.

The apples cooperate for the first time, even if they are organic. The first pile of organic apples actually looks okay in an eight and a half by eleven, but I decide to forfeit the extra money and have the interns do the touch-up work. I stand back from the print as it dries, trying to imagine the word *tempting* in a snakelike font, but my eyes can't adjust. I step closer to the picture, tripping over my bag. Developing fluid splashes on the table, ruining a stack of negatives from last month's ice cream cake campaign. The little boy smiles crooked, and his tongue slips out of his mouth a little on the left side. This isn't how I remember the picture. I pull the next one out to dry. The little boy's tongue is now sticking out, and his eyes are closed. I think for a minute I must have grabbed the wrong set. Even the apples are out of place, tumbling all over the foreground of the picture like they were kicked.

Someone knocks three quick, but jolly, raps on the door. "Hannah, you in there?" Miranda asks. I try to answer her, but all I can think is that Miranda knocks like Drew; something they must have learned as children. She knocks again, and I hold my breath. The words *come in* run soundlessly through my mind, and I can't move to open the door.

"Hannah," she says, "you just can't hide from this. We have to talk about this. My parents are livid. They want to see you, so you can call this thing off." Her voice shifts from jolly to irritated as she speaks. She puts too much emphasis on *off*, making it louder and last longer than it should as it escapes from her mouth. She jiggles the handle the proper number of times and the lock pops open, a safety feature in case of fire.

I cringe unsteadily into the tray of fluid below me. The note to the parents, I think, suddenly struck by the consequences. Miranda looks me up and down suspiciously. Her eyebrows furrow as she steps closer to me. She puts her face up close to mine, staring directly into my eyes.

"Hey H, you're not okay, are you? You shouldn't even be here."

"The organic apples, they're due today. Three o'clock," I say, looking down at myself, trying to see what she means. The floor feels unsteady and the red glow isn't helping.

"I need to go home," I say, crumbling down, cross-legged on the floor.

"You didn't turn the fan on, you haven't gotten any fresh air for almost an hour. Come on, get up. I'll take you home."

"The apples," I say. My lips go numb, and my body is exhausted.

Miranda leads me downstairs to the underground parking garage that only honchos get to park in. Her space is even reserved, which always makes people laugh, especially Drew. She drives an Escort, he would chuckle, an Escort with a reserved space in Manhattan. When we round the corner and step into the stall with her car, I smile a little. She puts me in the tiny backseat. The soft vinyl interior still smells new, and the carpets are immaculate.

She pulls abruptly out of the spot and begins the slow climb to street level. I press my face against the seat, reminded of trips my parents and I would take from Connecticut to Florida to see my father's parents. It would be so long, and after one full day I would be too comatose to even look out the window. I clutched the backseat like some kind of teddy bear, and every time the car began to slow, I crossed my fingers and hoped we were in Boca Raton. Miranda quickly accelerates out of the parking garage and into traffic. The car windows sputter mechanically down around me, and I shiver from the cool breeze through the tunnel, the brief drive through Hoboken, and up the stairs to my apartment.

"'Take a nap," she says. "I'll stay until you wake up."

I shut the bedroom door behind me, unable to say too much, embarrassed for being so stupid about the exhaust fan. My clothes stink of spilled fluid, so I fling open the closet to find something clean to wear. Finding absolutely clean clothes is a challenge, so I settle for the cleanest I have. Jeans and one of Drew's sweaters that shrunk to my size. It still smells like him, and I turn instinctively to see if he is there.

I can almost imagine him, feel his arms on my waist and the softness of his face against my neck. I will never feel that again, I think, breathing in his smell deeply, taking what little comfort I could from it. I throw myself down on the bed, rolling myself up in the blankets, breathing deeper and deeper. The smell of him wraps around me, fills me. I close my eyes and fall asleep, dreaming of a thousand mornings waking up next to him.

Cinnamon-streusel topping and the voices of Miranda and a man in the kitchen jar me from my slumber and beautiful dreams. I stumble out of my room and toward the kitchen door. I move quietly, looking at my feet and the floorboards, not wanting to be detected. Little down feathers cling to my knees and thighs. I think about ignoring them and going back to bed, but I realize that they are talking about me. I also realize that I can't expect tight-assed Randy, as Fox-Boy calls her, to be on my side. She was Drew's sister before she was my friend, and worst of all, she is Eleanor and Frederick's daughter. And even I know blood is thicker than water, no matter how dreadful the parents are.

Just as they coerced Drew into giving up bicycles, their parents withdrew Miranda from the Culinary Institute after her first week of classes. When she didn't return home of her own accord the first weekend after classes started, Eleanor drove from Mahwah to Pough-keepsie to bring her back. Frederick called the next day to arrange to get the tuition money back. How Miranda, or Drew for that matter, managed to accept those facts is beyond me, and it was never something to be discussed.

"So she showed up at work today a wreck?" he asks.

"Yeah, and she damn near fainted in the darkroom, forgot to turn on the ventilation fans. She's been sleeping since twelve o'clock."

"And she's been distraught over Drew's death?"

I push the door to the kitchen a little and peek through. Miranda is still dressed for work in one of her favorite power suits. Today's was her best, raw blue silk tailored exactly for her. It was cut just right so that you would notice simultaneously that she was a woman, and in charge. She leans back against the stove, assuming her deal-closing posture. She leans back the same way against the console table in her office when pitching an ad layout. She then turns her head and begins talking in a far-off way, as if what she had to say was some deep dark truth only we were meant to hear.

"Yes and no. I mean, what can you expect? She hasn't even been answering the phone since Friday. I can't tell what's going on. And then there's this whole business about the wedding on Saturday. My parents are in an uproar."

Ah, the truth, I say to myself, glad to have anticipated such treason from the woman who introduced me to Drew in the first place. I drop down lower to get a look at the bearded man at the table, expecting to find him drooling over her every word, the way most clients do when she gets that far-off look in her eye.

"Well, Miranda, it must be hard on everyone having to cancel such an important event. This adds a whole new dimension to the grieving process. The Bible tells us . . . " he starts. His words both settle my stomach, and for a moment, halt my treacherous friend.

Miranda leans forward from the stove and rests her elbows on the table just inches in front of him. She softens her voice as she interrupts, "But Pastor Joe, Hannah wants to go through with the wedding. Look, here's a receipt for the cake, dated Saturday. And my parents, really, who can't possibly understand."

"Really?" he asks, not sounding too excited.

"Miranda," I say, stepping inside the kitchen, "it's a

lovely cake, three tiers with natural white flowers for garnish. You would approve." Miranda went to the CIA to study pastry, but she was different then—lighter somehow—like angel-food cake. The smell of the cinnamon comes from a half-eaten bundt cake on the table. A confectioners' sugar glaze runs down either side of the cake like little rivers of snow. I slowly cut myself a piece and balance it on my hand as I break off still-warm pieces and greedily shove them in my mouth. "It's a shame you couldn't have made the cake. This is great."

Miranda stands up at the table looking alarmingly at the man called Pastor Joe, a middle-aged man with a graying beard and sharp blue eyes that seem to burst off of his face. He stands up as well, offering his pale, bony hand.

"Pastor Joe Koyla," he says. "First Church of Saints, Morristown."

I shove the rest of the cake into my mouth and wipe my hand on my leggings before offering it to him. Shaking his hand, I think I could crush it, and that I would crush it if the two of them were conspiring against me and my plans to go ahead with things. "So, Pastor, what brings you here?"

"Well, Hannah, you do. Miranda was telling me you might be having some trouble grieving. Grief is a process, and I could guide you through it if need be. It is my area of concentration."

Grief as a concentration, I think, how awful could that be, but his voice pulls me back in. He has a soft voice, the kind that lulled you into listening because you have to strain to hear him. He locks his hands together and leans back to cross his thin legs. "Tell me about this wedding," he says.

"What if I tell you I don't want to be talked out of it? Not by you or Miranda or Mr. and Mrs. Heinz."

"That would be fine," he says almost too sincerely with a smile. "Just tell me about your plans. I'm curious."

The sleep is starting to wear off, leaving me with a sick burning feeling in the bottom of my stomach. "My plans," I begin. "I ordered the cake, but you know that. There's the dress. The Manor was booked by Drew. That's one of those places that comes with everything except the couple and the cake. That's even what the brochure said, 'Everything but the couple and the cake.' That's about it. Enough?"

Pastor Joe uncrosses his legs and moves closer to the table, stretching his arms out like he is going to take a nap. He lowers his face directly in front of my down-turned eyes. "What if I tell you I think it's the best idea I've heard in a long time?"

I can't believe he just said that, and neither can Miranda, who drops the percolator into the sink, coffee grounds spilling on the floor and the counter. Her tough ad-lady facade washes down the drain with the coffee grounds. Her eyes are distorted and pained in the reflection off the dented-steel cabinet above the sink. She turns around to look at me directly, water dripping off her hands and down on her fine silk suit. I move to hand her a towel, but she wipes them down the front of her skirt.

He continues, cautiously looking over his shoulder at Miranda, "Hannah, you need to find peace with this man, however you think is best. Like I offered, I can guide you through the process, but we each have to decide what our process is. What is it you need to do?"

I am suddenly aware of a way I can disarm Miranda's weapon against me. "For the wedding," I start, doing my own cautious glancing at Miranda, "I need someone to officiate. I know we can't do a real ceremony. But someone to say something in the same vein."

"What do you mean, we can't do a real ceremony? These things are as you make them, Hannah. As we make them."

His comforting and soothing voice makes me realize how tired I still am. My eyes are heavy as I lay my head down on the table. Joe places a hand on my shoulder and begins to stroke it gently, kneading the knot that has been there for the last four days. To Miranda, he whispers, "Are you strong enough to be a part of this?"

"My parents, Joe, it'll kill them."

"Perhaps we can meet with them tomorrow, someplace neutral like my office."

I feel him stand up and put his coat on, but I can't bring myself to watch him leave. To watch him leave would be like seeing the magician's tricks. I want to put Pastor Joe someplace else in my mind, someplace safe where I could reach up and listen to his voice, and talk to him about Drew.

I want to confess that I was mad when he didn't get off the plane, because I thought he stayed over in Chicago on purpose to go to a ballgame or some bicycle convention. I cursed and cursed, frustrated that I had to wait for him to show up. And then he didn't show up. I want to tell Pastor Joe that it doesn't feel any different around here, that I was already moving so far away from Drew and our wedding, avoiding talking about it, avoiding doing anything about it. I want to tell him that I'm ashamed because every time for the last three months Drew looked up at me and smiled like a movie star, I suspected an ulterior wedding planning motive.

The weekend before he left, I came back from the market to find him playing one of my Strauss waltz discs. Scooping the produce bags out of my hands, he shuffled me toward the couch. He removed my shoes and socks and slipped the highest pair of heels I own onto my feet. I remember watching the short curls of his hair move in time with the music as he undid my laces. Jumping back, he hit the repeat play button on the CD player and presented himself to me in a Texas dip like some wayward debutante. I'd like to say we spent the evening in each other's arms, dancing waltzes around the couch, but we didn't. He drew me close to him, so close that I could smell the remnants of his morning aftershave. *I love dancing with you,* he whispered, before kissing my ears. *Yeah, sure you do,* I said, *you just don't want me to make a fool of you at the wedding.* He stopped holding me tightly for the rest of the waltz, and as the song ended, so did the dancing.

"I'll call you with a time," Miranda says.

I listen to the door shut, half pretending to myself that it is Miranda on her way out. Instead, she returns to the kitchen, pours herself a cup of coffee, and turns off the light. The television snaps on in the other room, and voices of the Home Shopping Network testimonial line fill the apartment. Someone gets a toot for buying a second item for a friend. The whole thing sounds so surreal, amplified through the kitchen table. I wonder when things would be normal again. If things would ever be normal again.

Perched on my favorite wooden stool in the darkroom of the latest agency to pay too much for my services, I wasn't thinking about the amount of money per hour I was wasting as my thoughts turned to Drew. My mind lingered on his fingers, thick and manly, covered with bicycle grease. Covered so consistently and often that no matter how many times you washed them, they still looked the same—their cuticles ringed in black like eyeliner. And I liked his fingers that way; it gave them life, showed that they did something, that maybe they could take charge. I would like them to take charge. Take charge of me. My body. My breasts. I would like to kiss his knuckles and his wrists and his arms before they circled me and our bodies became one. I wanted him, dirty fingers and all.

After six months, desire of this magnitude was not to be trifled with. Rena, in fact, couldn't understand why two people who liked each other enough to eat out almost every night didn't have sex within two dates. I tried explaining to her, and to myself, that it had precisely to do with the fact that we did like each other enough to have dinner every night. He even talked to me about it once. "H," he said, "we could, you know, and it would probably be a mind-blowing experience, but letting it build up could be just as cool. I have serious intentions here. I like you."

At the time, I didn't question his serious intentions; they at once scared the bejesus out of me, and made me feel oddly comforted like maybe, just maybe, he could be the one person to stay. With me. For me. No matter what or who came along. At night, sleeping by myself, after the proverbial cold shower, it was the echo of his "serious intentions" that put a smile on my lips and dreams in my head, and gave me the confidence to meet him halfway.

Today, what I wanted had nothing to do with serious intentions or falling in love; it had to with those hands, those greasy hands, and my thighs. Or perhaps his lips, soft and pink and full, and my thighs. Rena would be proud, and I resolved to do something to be proud of and satisfied with myself.

None of our "dates," if you could call them that, were

planned more than a few hours ahead of time, even though I saw him just about every day. I would call him or he would call me, and whoever called would say something like, *How about Chinese for dinner,* as casually as if we were living together, or already had plans to meet. These calls always came early in the day—well before most even considered dinner. Heck, some people were still finishing their breakfast latte. I took this as a good sign.

Tonight, my roommate was out of town, and I thought after six months of restaurants I would cook. Not that I knew how to, but I figured I could try. And in doing so, get him into my apartment and quite possibly my bed.

I called him early, earlier than usual. "Turkey dinner at my place tonight?" I blurted out, excited.

"Yeah," he said, "with stuffing and cranberry sauce?"

"Anything for you," I cooed, hoping he'd get the innuendo.

"Anything?" he replied in a sly voice. "I could go for anything."

With the stage set and my anticipation high, I left the darkroom early and headed out to the grocery and Victoria's Secret. I pick up a turkey breast, stuffing, some potatoes, carrots, cranberry sauce, a Mrs. Smith's Apple Pie, and a bra and panty set that could be comfortably worn under clothes yet still offer a sexy surprise.

By the time I got home it was close to five. I cut up the carrots and the potatoes, added broth to the stuffing mixture, and flipped over the turkey breast to read the directions. Microwave defrost on low for an hour, then roast in oven at 350 for twenty minutes per pound. The breast weighed close to ten pounds. And was partially frozen. That would mean one hour in the microwave and three hours and twenty minutes in the oven. The clock over the stove read six o'clock.

What the heck, I figured, and began microwaving the bird. Drew knocked on my door twenty minutes later. I still hadn't changed into my Victoria's Secret purchases. I opened it, reluctantly, and was greeted with one of those one cheek then the other cheek series of kisses that French people exchange. His lips lingered just a little below each of my earlobes. "That's for anything," he said, handing me a bottle of white zinfandel, "and this is to help it along."

The sensation of his breath on my neck was enough to move anything along, although I didn't want to tell him that and ruin the surprise. Instead, I motioned toward the microwave and turkey breast rotating inside it and said, "Dinner's going to be on the late side. Hope you don't mind?"

"If I get hungry, can I eat you instead?" he asked, the glint from the candle I lit to kill cooking odors reflecting off his smile like stage lights on a pageant contestant.

I decided to go with it. I extended my hand out toward him. "Appetizer?"

He kissed it. "Tempting, but I feel I should let my appetite build. I was never one to spoil my dinner. I honestly believe that good things come to those who wait. Wine?"

He scooped up the bottle and proceeded across the room to the couch. I picked up the corkscrew and the glasses, and joined him after turning off the carrots and the potatoes. How easy, I thought, how nice.

Draining the bottle of wine, we talked and talked and talked. We talked as if we hadn't just spent the last six months going to dinner all over the five boroughs and most of northern New Jersey. I asked him about his first kiss—a girl at camp. I asked him about his best kiss—he said me at the door. He asked me about the picture of the guy on my fridge. Old boyfriend? he questioned—ad campaign, I replied. Our questions circled around sex, a subject we never really broached before.

"First time?" Drew asked quietly, as if he might not want to know.

I considered telling him never, but opted for honesty. "Senior prom," I said, not wanting to offer names or details. "You?" I added, shifting the question uncomfortably back to him.

"Senior year," he said. "College."

Luckily, before it could get worse, the buzzer for the

turkey went off. Instead of setting the table, we stood in the kitchen buffet-style and loaded our plates from the pans. We must have loaded them two or three times over. We ate so much that moving back to the couch took too much effort. Groaning like wounded animals, we laid down together and soon fell fast asleep.

Whether it was the meal or the company, it was the best sleep of my life. His chest moved lightly, and every muscle of his body seemed to melt into the couch. He was so peaceful and relaxed that it wore off on me. For the first time, I didn't feel like I had to worry about waking up and finding him gone or different. His smile didn't even change in his sleep.

In the morning, I woke up to find his hand, the hand of the magical fingers, on my chest, like a present. I didn't even get up to wrap myself in Victoria's secrets. I pressed my lips on his hand, on each finger, his palm, his wrist, up his arm. I kissed his neck and his ear, and as I made it to his lips, his eyes fluttered up like magic.

He slid his fingers around the back of my head and pulled my face closer to his. Our lips melted together and connected our bodies so completely that I would die if we stopped there. Every nerve in my body was screaming for attention from his lips. And his lips were more than ready to comply.

He undid the buttons to my shirt with one hand and slipped my skirt off with the other. My clothes fell silently to the floor, followed by his. He smiled his movie-star smile, but he didn't say a word. Pressed against his body, the soft brown curls of his chest hair, the warmth of him, I found a heaven I never thought existed. I closed my eyes and let his lips cover me. I rested my head back, relaxed for the first time in years, and let it happen. Let us happen.

Wednesday, October 22, 1997

I wake up by the time the sun has progressed halfway across the kitchen. It is close to noon. This new capacity for sleeping, but remaining tired, amazes me. Ruby would call this classic avoidance, and I would call her to hear her say so, but she calls me first.

"Let me bring you something," she says. "Miranda called last night, told me about you in the darkroom and you in the kitchen."

I check the living room for Miranda, but find only an empty coffee cup and a book misplaced on the coffee table. She probably had to go into work. "This isn't something to make a big deal over. I'm just tired. Really tired." I hear the words and almost believe them. After all, I am tired but not just tired. I hope she wouldn't catch the omission.

"I'm coming over and bringing you some lunch. Maybe some seafood bisque from that shop you liked so much on Witherspoon. Just be there, okay. No more disappearing acts. And I want you to be presentable tonight."

"Tonight?" I ask.

"Yes," she says. "Drew's parents and that pastor in Morristown. Some sort of remediation or mediation."

"Remediation?" I ask.

"Or mediation, yes. Something about the wedding and getting you to stop it. Miranda said you knew this, is your mind going, too? Or have you been drinking? I won't judge, just tell me the truth."

"No," I say, "just come if you're going to. I might have things to do."

I stretch myself from the kitchen table and think of things I might have to do. Water the plants. Take a shower. Return phone calls. Find shoes for the dress. Water the plants I missed on Sunday. I decide to water the plants.

The plants were a concession with Drew, being that I wanted a cat. He said if I could talk to them, keep them alive, then maybe we'd discuss a cat, even though he preferred dogs. I told him plants are not fuzzy or cute. He brought home a dozen African violets in full bloom, both fuzzy and cute, which we arranged in the living room. So I talk to them as I water them, rotating their positions around the windowsills, so each one had some full-blown sun time and some shade time. I stroke their leaves, relishing their soft velvet feel under my fingertips, grateful to have something that still needs me.

"*Alouette, Alouette, je te plumerai, je te plumerai la tête, je te plumerai le dos, et la tête, et le dos*—" I sing as I remove the dead leaves; the doorbell rings in the middle of the second chorus.

I think at once that it must be my mother, so I breeze by the door, open it, and walk away into the kitchen to put on some coffee.

"Girl, you are one kind of mess," Fox-Boy says, stepping into the kitchen with his hands full of dead violet leaves. "Miranda said you weren't doing so good on your own. What's the deal?"

I stop making coffee. "Let's go get some coffee," I say. "Two lattes and some plant food for my friends."

"Whatever makes you happy," Fox-Boy says, making me all too glad he knocked on my door.

The lunchtimers are on the street, rushing from sidewalk bar to sidewalk bar in search of the perfect table, the perfect fat-free meal, or just someplace that doesn't have a wait. When I would call out sick from work to play hooky at home, I was always amazed at the lunch crowd. Judging by the number, you would have thought people actually took the Path train back to eat. No way could that many people work in the few offices or the many shops that lined the streets. Fox-Boy leads us through the crowd, his height of six foot two aiding him in the process. Every few steps, he turns to make sure I am still keeping up.

"Let's go to the Coffee Grind, they make good latte," I say.

"Do you hear yourself, H? They make good latte. Is that what your life out here has become? Good latte?"

Fox-Boy still lives in the Village, not even a trendy part, and considered it to be the be-all and end-all of his existence and everyone else's. That's where he became Fox-Boy instead of John. When he was John, people felt free to tack Boy onto the end of it and make Walton jokes. Then a kind young lady, desperately and hopelessly in love with John-Boy, namely Rena, named him Fox-Boy. She told me over the phone one afternoon, shortly after figuring John was a hopeless endeavor, that he was just so foxy, her own Fox-Boy. She made the mistake of telling him, too. He then told everyone else, becoming hopelessly indebted to and a faithful companion of Rena. Rena was holding out for more than companionship, but Fox-Boy wasn't giving in anytime soon. He liked being foxy too much to be in any one person's foxhole.

"There's nothing wrong with latte. And what happened to helping me? And what about Rena?"

"Rena will blow over, you shocked her, and she

never thought you were one to go around shocking people. But see, I am helping you. I calmed her down, even got her to say she'd come. Now, H—"

"Yeah, she told me, too, but really she told me I was nuts. Is she really going to come?"

"Yes," he says drawing out the *s* like a child mimicking a snake. "She'll even wear a bridesmaid dress. Can I pleassssse finissssh?"

"Really?" I say. "Thanks."

"Now really, there is a time for wallowing in your latte, crying over steamed milk, and a time to carpe diem."

"Fox-Boy, you rehearsed that line."

"No, no, it just came to me. Carpe diem. Simple as that. I don't plan conversations."

"Drew hasn't even been gone a month yet, and you want me to seize the day. Seize this," I say, flipping him off.

"Testy, testy. I meant you had a wedding to plan. You aren't the only one who lost Drew, you know."

"Yeah. Just wait until Mr. and Mrs. Heinz ambush me tonight. In public, at this church. Get this. I found a pastor to do the ceremony. Actually, Miranda did."

Fox-Boy's mouth hangs open like he is waiting for a spoon of something as he holds open the Coffee Grind's door. "Tight-ass Randy found you a freethinker, talk about role reversal."

"Don't call her that. Anyway, it's not like she knew that was what she was doing. She thought he was a grief management counselor." I think for a few minutes about how tight-assed Miranda really can be, how she has briefcases to match her shoes, only shops retail, and took classes on how to use her day planner. "I guess it is funny," I say.

He looks at me and rolls his eyes.

"Okay," I say, "very funny."

He orders two lattes and points out the biscotti to me. I shake my head no, as I try to squeeze into the table nearest the window without knocking over the huge pile of shopping bags surrounding two women and a three-year-old having hot chocolates and mini-quiche.

"Excuse me," I say, knocking one small bag to the side.

The toddler wanders off his chair and into the back; the mother does not even move to see where he is headed. Fox-Boy clicks his tongue ring at them in a sort of modern *tsk, tsk,* as he squeezes past to sit down.

"Why are some people allowed to procreate and people like me must walk this world alone? Will the wonders ever cease?"

"Stop being so damn self-important and maybe I'll carpe the day or whatever it is you want me to do."

"I want you to drink your latte and let me give you a facial. Rena and I got this great new stuff. Works wonders for the bride-to-be. Must be perfect or everyone will talk."

"As if they aren't going to be talking already?"

I set my cup down too hard and latte spills over onto the table. It is something I could cry about, but Fox-Boy would have never allowed it. He would say something about my mascara. Or how it made him look in public. And I would laugh, almost like a hyena. And then feel guilty. It is too soon to laugh, I think.

"As if we care," Fox-Boy says. "Just screw it and them. Tell that to Ellie and Freddie, or Mr. and Mrs. Heinz, as you prefer."

Ellie and Freddie, I think. They are people I never met. If an Ellie or a Freddie lurks somewhere in the shadows of Eleanor and Frederick Heinz, I would be shocked. Watching those two in action during family gatherings and various holiday occasions over the last four years only strengthened my opinion that marriage changes things. You couldn't tell me that people that unhappy would have seen fit to be married that way. I'm not saying I blamed either one of them; all I'm saying is that combined they make for a pretty twisted picture of wedded bliss. Drew never understood this as evidence for my side, electing instead to believe it was the stress of retirement, that they were just getting used to each other again. *After thirty-five years,* I said to him, *getting used to what?* He never had an answer no matter how many times I pushed the subject. Most people like to believe in their parents. Put them on some pedestal for exemplary conduct. I couldn't do that with Ruby, and I certainly wasn't going to do it with Mr. and Mrs. Heinz.

"They will remain Mr. and Mrs. Heinz to me, thanks. Any more personal than that and my well-being would file a restraining order. They trouble me."

"Well, H, they're about to trouble you a little more." He finishes off his latte with a large swig. "How about that facial?" He stands up and makes a sweeping gesture toward the door. Through the glass, I see the street has quieted down a little, so I sip the last of my latte and breeze as gracefully as I can under his arm and out onto the street.

Back in my apartment, after complaining about using the stairs, he prepares the face batter, as the packet directed, demanding that I sit and try to think nonwrinkling thoughts for the fifteen minutes it takes the goo to setup. Fox-Boy begins massaging my feet and the backs of my calves. He fancies himself a healer because he once dated a masseuse. I could never find out what kind of masseuse, if it was on the level or a little more Bowery, but his hands feel good, solid and warm, melting some of the tension out of me. The avocado goo also does its part to work away tension with its coolness settling on my face, but lifting and tightening it as well. I'm melting, I think.

My Intended

The last time I felt this free was in the Gulf of Mexico, the warm salty water buoying my overworked body up against Drew, who stood shark-guard while I floated, lifelessly relaxing. He told me I was moaning with pleasure the entire time my ears were underwater. *Liar,* I said, splashing him, starting the best splash fight I ever had, including three years at summer camp and three years as a counselor. Afterward, he carried me out of the water and into the bedroom of the mock–Old South bedroom, complete with mosquito netting. I told Fox-Boy about this, and he smiled at me, massaging my scalp.

"I'm really going to miss that," I say, thinking about all the other vacations, all of the motel and hotel bedrooms, thinking about our own bed in the other room. I can't quite believe that I'll never share a bed with him again. That I'll never touch him, hear him breathe, or feel the heat coming off his body. The thought strikes me as very cold, quiet, and lonely.

"Remember away," he says, "it's the only thing that will help."

He begins the slow process of peeling away the wrap, just as my mother bursts in bearing gifts of sourdough bread and New England clam chowder. "Comfort food," she says, hustling in through the door.

Seeing Fox-Boy, my facial mask, and me on the couch, she drops her packages along with her jaw. "Just what in God's green earth do you think you are doing?

This is completely unacceptable. Hannah, get away from that man."

The facial must not have registered with her yet, so I lean my head around Fox-Boy to look at her. "Can't he take the facial off first?"

"Oh, oh. Fox-Boy. I didn't realize."

"Yes, hello, Ruby. Or should I call you Jack Ruby, always expecting the worst. Shoot first, ask questions later? You need a facial, too, I suppose. Everyone needs to lighten up. Drew would not appreciate such a bunch of high-strung, tense women."

"Quit it," I say, "take the mask off. It's starting to hurt."

It is one of those scenes people dread, their mother hovering around while they try to extricate themselves from trouble caused by themselves and friends. I feel delinquent. Ruby passes through the living room, looking for this or that, as she heats up the soup, makes a salad, and sets the table for lunch. She pauses at the side of the couch, shakes her head, and moves on. Fox-Boy struggles with the avocado goo, trying to free it from my earlobes. It tightened my skin all right, tightened it until it burns.

Frantically, he dials Rena, with all the exasperation of a beauty queen's mother. "Rena," he shouts into the speakerphone, fully expecting her groggy self to answer.

The Pussy Cat Lounge really makes a bear of her in the morning.

"Yes, Boy," she answers, "and you would need . . . ?" Her tone seemingly indicates a slight stress to their relationship. She is not happy to be hearing from him at this moment. It is a tone I am familiar with, though usually it is a tone Miranda would use with her men friends.

"The antidote for the avocado mask. It seems to not be willing to relinquish itself from Hannah's earlobes."

"Really, John, it was meant for the T-zone only. Oily areas. Try cold water with one part lemon juice. That should cut it."

"Well, thank you, crown princess of doom. What, no luck last night?" Fox-Boy asks in the most sarcastic tone I have ever heard him use with her.

They're still arguing about her working at the bar, I realize. "Let me go check on Ruby," I say, excusing myself from the living room.

"It seems Fox-Boy and Rena are having a lovers' quarrel," I mention to Ruby as she washes and tears spinach leaves from their stems.

"But I thought, he was, you know." She tries nodding her head to gesture in some way, so as not to offend or to say it out loud.

"He might be, but he doesn't want to limit his

choices. You do, after all, fall in love with who you happen to fall in love with. No rules for that."

"Is that healthy? With, well, you know."

"Ruby, please. Not everyone left their common sense on the bus. Just because he leaves his choices open doesn't mean he takes chances. Ask him if you're so worried."

"I couldn't do that. It wouldn't be proper." She gets huffy with the spinach, fluffing it dry and into a bowl, throwing the hard-boiled eggs at it.

"Then don't worry about it. All I was saying is that he and Rena are arguing like lovebirds about her meeting other people. That's all. Just a little gossip."

"Well, okay, I guess I like gossip."

"Yeah, I guess you do, Ms. I Tape Soap Operas," I say, laughing.

Ruby laughs, too, and Fox-Boy walks in to find us both laughing. He cackles heartily back at us. It feels so good to just let it out, let out all the funny things I had seen and heard over the last twenty-odd days. All the people coming and going around me tiptoeing on eggshells like I was going to snap any minute. I should have snapped, I think, making myself laugh so hard that I start to cry.

Fox-Boy and Ruby stop to look at me, pressing their hands on my shoulders. I let the tears rolls down my cheeks in big fat drops like spring rain. They roll down my shirt and into my lap where they dissolve. I let them. I let them. And I let them.

By the time I stop, the soup is cold and needs to be microwaved back to warm. The thin metallic beep startles me. I can't handle being so far away from someone that I cared about as much I cared about Drew. So far that I can't even shout out his name, or send him a letter to tell him how much I love him. I never wanted to lose anything, and stood such a protective watch over it all; yet now, I look around and none of my guarding has done any good. The phone won't ring and take it all back.

Fox-Boy places a bowl of soup in front of me, and Ruby pours me some tomato juice. "If you don't eat anything, I'm going to make you drink something," she says.

"Whatever," I say, trying to feed myself without spilling it all over. Soup feels good in my mouth, warm and filling. I realize I haven't been eating near enough. I used to eat all the time, anywhere from three to five meals a day depending on where I happened to be and whether or not there was ice cream nearby.

"Ice cream," I say, dropping the spoon in the empty bowl. "I could use some ice cream." A little soup spills out of the corner of my mouth before I am through speaking. I lick at it with my tongue and feel suddenly like I am four or five.

"Honey, we all could use a little ice cream," Fox-Boy says, opening the freezer, finding none. "Ruby, whaddaya say, we go fetch the girl some dessert?"

"Ah, I don't know if she should be—"

"I can be alone, go with him. Fox-Boy doesn't like to go anywhere unescorted."

Ruby looks at me, sizing up whether or not I'm going to stay in the apartment without them in it.

"Look at my hair, really, let me get a shower and then we can start doing the seating chart. The place said they need the list by Wednesday to have the little cards printed. Really, do go with him."

"Really," Fox-Boy says, taking Ruby's hands to his lips.

When the door finally shuts behind them, a weight is lifted off my chest. Instead of feeling like someone was pulled away from me, I feel suddenly aware of the warmth in the room. I look over at the chair where Drew used to sit, and I can almost see him there, not physically, but in my mind. He smiles and reaches his hand over toward me. His fingers hang there in the air, moving slightly as if blown by a breeze, trying to reach me. I watch the tension form in his wrist. I study its thin blue lines and the pink fleshy color of his palm. His hands look warm, alive. I reach out to touch him, to hold his hand like I used to in the car. I grab his index finger in mine, and instead of feeling him and his soft warm skin, I feel cold, like I am holding ice. I open my hands and turn away. I rub my hands over my eyes to shake the image of him, and spring from my seat heading for the shower to wash it off.

Standing under the stream of hot water, the soap washes itself down off me and around my feet. I watch the bubbles foam up briefly and disappear like so many other things. The air is heavy with steam and chokes down my throat. After ten minutes, I know I should get out, but can't. I take Drew's can of shaving cream from the ledge of the tub and spray a little of the aqua-green gel into my hand. I am surprised when it poufs up into a white foam. I smear it up and down my legs in an attempt to shave what I haven't in about a month and a half. I am trying for tonight, for the pastor and Miranda and the dreadful Mrs. Heinz. I take his straight razor, the one without the dainty pink, leg-protecting wires, and begin to scrape quickly, because the water is running cold; even the steam is dissipating. The cold water falls in fat drops and runs little rivers into the shaving cream. I spread more on, and more rivers form. I go faster with the razor, bulging my calf out as I turn my leg to the side. I scrape the razor up and around the bulb of my calf, slicing it nearly the whole way. A thick stream of blood spills over my calf, around my ankle, and pools at the base of my heel. I watch my blood mix with the water and swirl like the bubbles down the drain. I wince with the sting of the water on the cut, but I don't move. The tide of red holds me in my place as goose bumps cover me. It would be so easy, I think.

"So—" I start to say to myself, stopping as the chain on the front door swings back into place.

I quickly dry off and tack several bandages on my leg. They help for a few minutes, but blood still seeps around their edges. I choose to ignore it and step inside my closet to get dressed. I pull on a navy-blue peasant dress that would provoke the least amount of attention from Eleanor and Frederick. The clock on the bedside table tells me my meeting with them and the Pastor may be only an hour away. I can't be sure though; I'm not sure which clocks actually keep good time. It was something Drew kept track of in an attempt to make sure he was never late for anything. Ruby and Fox-Boy sit together in the living room, watching Oprah talk to some super-model about being a superperson. Together, they attack her clothes, hair, and makeup with rapid-fire bursts like gunfire on an open field of hostile enemies. I suppress a laugh.

"How this?" I ask, spinning around in front of them.

"Conservative. *Très* conservative," Fox-Boy says.

"Very nice, dear," Ruby adds, not taking her eyes off the television.

Then they both start to laugh. "Quit it, I'm going to that church thing. Remember, the ambush."

In unison, they reply, "Oh, it's fine. Good choice." Ruby purses her lips together, trying to keep from saying more.

"Just say it, Ruby."

"Fine, okay, I won't mince words. But why in the hell can't these people leave you alone? Let you do what you have to."

"Why can't they go to hell?" Fox-Boy asks.

I turn and leave the room in search of a clip to pull back my hair. "Will you drive me, Ruby? Morristown?"

"Of course, I wouldn't let you face these people alone."

From the bathroom, I hear her start in on these people and the many atrocities they have committed against both her and me, not to mention poor Miranda and Drew, starting from day one, five years ago. Ruby's capacity for remembering such details about people's behavior with regard to unreturned dinner invitations, unaccommodating holiday plans, and downright rudeness at social gatherings amazes me.

It's my job, she told me once, shortly after marrying Allen. *Faculty wives talk, that's what they do. Scheme, Mother, faculty wives scheme,* I said, knowing all too well what she meant from my own brief forays into the world of the intelligentsia social gatherings the year Ruby and McEllory, God bless his soul, were living in Prague, and I had no home for the holidays. The president of the university and his wife had all the foundlings in: the students with no homes, the foreign faculty, the faculty trying to get ahead. I never heard more people say publish or perish in my entire life. It was like they all read the same secret manifesto and couldn't dislodge it from memory. When Ruby married Allen, I worried he might be one of them, never doubting for a moment that Ruby would easily adapt into the role of high priestess of the Economics Department if the situation arose.

"But social issues aside, Mr. Fox-Boy. The stunt these people are trying to pull off now simply must be stopped. No one said they had to come to the damn thing." Ruby finishes off her glass of orange juice like it was something stronger, perhaps wishing it were something stronger.

"I hear you, sister. Those people wouldn't even share a car with us to get to the funeral. 'We have it fine, er, young man,' he said, looking down at his wife as if she was going to crack for having to speak with me and Rena. As if, I wanted to tell her. Big fat as if."

I didn't know they had been rude to Fox-Boy and Rena at the funeral; I hadn't really noticed anything at all that day. How slipshod of me to not be looking out for them. "I'm so sorry, John," I call out from the bathroom, trying to find the other piece to my hair clip. "I can't say I don't believe it, I'm just sorry I didn't know until now."

"No skin off my nose. That's what nose rings are for." He snorts.

"So that's why," Ruby says, like she is really considering the idea. Maybe there was something stronger in her orange juice. I decide not to ask; it would be better if I don't know.

"Can we go now? The last thing I want to be is late."

Ruby smoothes down her sensible navy skirt that I hadn't realized she was wearing, touches up her lipstick, and smiles at me. "Let's roll."

"Fuck 'em," Fox-Boy shouts at us through the closing door.

Fuck them, I think, turning the words around in my mind, knowing that saying it would be much easier than doing it.

I try to sleep on the way out to Morristown, not wanting to see all the neat lawns and houses with gingerbread trim. Drew always pointed out that this was where the stockbrokers, like himself, and their wives, meaning me, went to live when they were tired of not having a place to park their Saabs or grill salmon steaks on Sunday afternoons. He would beam proudly through neighborhoods, swiveling his head from side to side like a cop on patrol. *These are my people,* he would say, *welcome.*

Pastor Joe's church is not one to disappoint the neighborhood. Rustic stone with circular driveway. Pine archway, stained-glass side panels, oak pews. Everything that could be expected of a church in a historically wealthy area. Pastor Joe must be an anomaly to the church then. Long before Drew died, Miranda told me about this pastor she knew who did all kinds of charity work, rarely having the time to preach to the congregation that supported him. She also told me he feels the sick and the poor need him more than the good wives of Morristown, and that his example meant more that any sermon he could write down. I respect that ideal even more now, seeing exactly what kind of comforts he left behind when he headed out to preach to the masses.

A man approaches us from the shadows, and I fail to realize it is Joe until he is right in front of me, shaking Ruby's hand. He traded his civilian clothes for the more traditional collared look. "For the show," he says, winking at me with a finger under his collar. "The others are in my study."

The thought of the others makes me shiver. This face-off was a bad idea. They could have just sent a nasty note back to me, told Miranda never to speak to me, whatever, just anything but this. They didn't need to bring God into it. Or Pastor Joe. We follow him down a winding corridor to a door painted hot pink. "My office," he says, pushing it in, revealing Miranda, Eleanor, and Frederick. Miranda sits far away from them, going so far as to lean over the farthest arm of her chair to escape them. She is on their side, yes, but nowhere near happy about it. She avoids looking at me, choosing instead to stare at the carpet, inspect her polished navy pumps. I think about how she used to be my friend, and that blood really is thicker than water.

"Might we start with a prayer?" Pastor Joe asks, bowing his head to begin before receiving a response.

Mrs. Heinz clears her throat, "Father, couldn't we just get this thing over with. Have the matter at hand dispelled. This really isn't the time for prayer."

However unconventional Pastor Joe is, hearing someone say that it isn't the time for prayer triggers something. He squeezes my shoulder and looks Mrs. Heinz dead in the eye. "Fine then," he says. "Hannah and I thought you might want to be included in the planning of the ceremony that we will hold on Saturday to remember your son and to exclaim the covenant bond that is between two people when they decide to marry. You see, marriage, I believe, is not the big church ceremony with the frilly dress and the priest in full vestments; marriage is the decision that is made in two people's hearts when they support and love one another and decide to make that commitment known to the world."

"I must stop you right there, Father—"

"Pastor Joe, please," he quickly corrects.

"Fine, Pastor Joe, you say 'will hold'? I thought we came to discuss the surety of this whole matter. I don't see 'will hold' as an uncertain term."

Mrs. Heinz's formal training in linguistics is paying off for her at the price of Mr. Heinz, who remains stock-still, hand over his eyes, trying to hide the embarrassment reddening his face. Miranda shifts uncomfortably. Watching her writhe in her seat, the imitation leather cracking under her, I decide to not be mad at her. To let it go. To let it all go.

"That is because there is no uncertainty, no law that requires your permission, no covenant broken. This is between Hannah, Drew, and God. I thought you came tonight to be supportive of this end. Supportive of bringing the love your son had for this woman to life in the world now, despite everything."

"I'm not going to sit through this," she says, looking at Frederick, grabbing behind her chair for her purse. "I had it with this girl long before now, and I don't have to put up with this insult at a time like this. Fred, Miranda?"

Frederick is quick to his feet, from years of practice, I guess. I have seen him scurry after her at least half a dozen times. Our engagement announcement, when Drew's aunt Riva decided to serve ham instead of turkey at Thanksgiving, when Miranda withdrew in the middle of her last MBA semester, and when she found a bicycle catalog with Drew's Series 7 manual, among many others. I am overwhelmed by the desire to touch Mr. Heinz, to apologize. I try to make eye contact, but he turns away. Miranda takes her time with her purse, digging through to get her car keys. *Sorry,* she whispers to me, walking past and through the hot pink door, which Fred is holding open, Eleanor long since past.

Their multicolored forms move fuzzily through the stained glass behind Joe's desk. Fred rushes over the lawn, his long legs taking wide steps. A late-model Buick pulls up to the curb, and Fred gets in the passenger side. Miranda opens the door behind her father, stares for a minute at the church, then gets in. I watch the Buick disappear around the bend in the parking lot. I have a hard time imagining Drew as part of that group. He wasn't one to storm out of the room, let alone a town. I imagine he would lean back and laugh at this scene. It would be so funny to him that he would slap his thighs, like a bird trying to take off and snort every few minutes to get air. He would raise his hand up for me to give him a high-five.

The three of us sit very still, looking at the vacant chairs around us for signs of something, hoping almost that for some reason they might return. "That didn't go well," Joe says, popping the white tab out of his collar. "Let's talk about what you want."

"I'm not so sure," I say, wincing at how stupid I must sound.

"Surely you know something, or you wouldn't be here right now. Think about it. What do you want to say to Drew?"

His words turn over and upside down in my mind. I want to say a lot of things to Drew. I want to shout out to him, *I'm over here* and *Come back,* like a mother would shout to a lost child. *Come back,* I would shout until my voice is hoarse and my throat aching. *I love you,* I would scream, making sure everyone heard. "I want him to know all the things I held back. I did hold back, you know. I never let him know how much I cared. Sure I said I loved him, but I never once said I loved him and only him, that he was my world. In fact, I fought him knowing, tried to cover it up, hide it. If I said it, I was convinced it would all disappear," I say, my throat going dry. I cough a few times, stop, and then cough some more, little tears squeezing out of my eyes.

Pastor Joe leans across his desk closer to me. "What if I say you could do the whole shebang? The real deal?"

"Real deal?" Ruby asks, leaning forward with a conspiratorial grin on her face.

"Yes, the real deal. The service with vows and offerings. Take a look at the standard setup." He pushes a pamphlet across the desk to me; Services in Love is written in gold cursive letters across a printed bouquet of white roses. He winks like a car salesman as I look back up at him. "Just take a look and circle the parts you're interested in. I do this with all my couples, why should you be any different?"

I smile at that idea. Why should I be any different?

Why shouldn't I have a wedding if I am planning a wedding? I take the pamphlet and stick it in my purse.

Joe extends his hand to Ruby as we stand. "Peace be with you," he says.

"Also with you," she says, her schooling in the many religious customs of her previous spouses paying off.

Joe then takes both my hands in his warm sweaty palms. "I'm so glad you came, Hannah, I'll call you in a day or two."

Thursday, October 23, 1997

Getting Ruby to leave is a feat I am not up to and that ultimately works to my advantage. I wake up to the smells of coffee, bacon, and her special French toast roasting in a maple glaze in the oven. She greets me in the middle of a train of thought.

"Just wonderful to live near all those stores. Pulled on sneakers, hit the street, found everything I would need to cook a dinner party for thirty. I must tell Allen how wonderful this is. All the little shops with little shop-keepers. Just wonderful. Good morning, Hannah."

Morning, just wonderful. One of the pleasures of working is the ability and necessity to fill up entire days with a specific activity. Even if you had nothing planned, you at least knew that your presence was required for a large chunk of the day. Both fortunately and unfortunately my schedule as a freelancer allows me time—lots of time. I can't bear to think of how to fill my days this week, even with the Saturday still left to be planned, or how to spend next week, alone again in an empty apartment.

I pick up the wedding services pamphlet from the table next to the couch. I flip it over and read the raised gilded letters on the back. *Your wedding day will be one of the most memorable days of your life. Your vows should be delivered wherever your heart desires. Be married by someone who really cares!* I wonder if Joe wrote that or if the whole thing came as a package deal. I drop the pamphlet back down on the table, not quite ready to make those kinds of decisions. I will handle it later, I tell myself, looking around the room to find something else to do, as if I had so many other things to do. "I need a pet," I say to Ruby in the other room. "Something to be with me."

"But, dear, I'm here," she says flatly, like she wasn't ever going to leave. As if she has stood by my side every minute of every day since my birth, forsaking all others to be my mother and my mother alone. Big fat as if.

"And when Allen returns, where will you go? You may be his pet, but not mine," I shout to her in the kitchen.

"Really now, is that the kind of thing to say? I will simply refuse to be a part of it. Come eat."

I look over at Drew's chair; an old copy of the *Wall*

Street Journal peaks out from under the upholstered skirt. I can't imagine picking that paper up and throwing it away. He always took care of his things; it was a rule we had so that no one accidentally lost something important to them. No one was supposed to lose anything. We promised that about a half a dozen times, and he isn't keeping up his part of the deal. Using my toe, I drag the paper out a little more. Bill Gates and Alan Greenspan stare stippled grimaces up at me before I push them all the way under and head into the kitchen.

Ruby sets a plate of French toast and bacon in front of me, which I look at for a while, unsure whether or not I feel like eating. The syrup forms a perfectly round pool under the French toast and edges up against the strips of bacon that rest on either side like it was made by some short-order chef in a diner. I stick my fork in the thick syrup and draw its tines around to make four-lane highways around the French toast. Connecting one end of the highway to the other is impossible though; the sticky mess of syrup collapses in on itself before I can even turn the fork around.

Slicing off some French toast and chewing it slowly, I try to think of the things I need to do. Dress have. Cake ordered. Guests reinvited. Hall, food, and entertainment, Drew finished. Pastor Joe, I think, *be married by someone who cares*. But I don't know what to do with that thought or the memory of his hands surrounding mine. There was something that was at once familiar and at once strange about him. Like he knew me, but I couldn't remember where we met. I run over the list again. Cake, dress, guests, hall. Cake, dress, guests, hall. With my mouth full, I finally say aloud "table chart," grateful to have it be something other than Joe.

"No, actually, I took the liberty of doing that this morning. I counted up how many people said they're going to come, phoned that into the hall, and said to hell with telling people where to sit. Very freeing experience." Ruby looks proudly at me, smiling, slaps her hand against the table, almost upsetting the syrup bottle. "Damn freeing."

Very freeing experience; I try to figure out if I am mad or not. I want to be in control of this, and here she is phoning the catering hall, The Wedding Bell Manor, and telling them to hell with the seating chart. That was my place, my thing to do. But it is done, completed, and finished. My responsibilities, aside from getting there and dealing with Pastor Joe, are over. I could hug her for that. I am actually going through with the wedding, and my mother, Ruby the self-absorbed, is willingly helping me. "Thanks. I'm glad it's all over with." I say, knowing my voice probably doesn't sound sincere. Sincerity being one of the harder emotions to get back after Drew's passing.

"Really, thanks," I say again after a minute of staring at a piece of bacon between my fingertips.

"But that's not all. You need shoes and makeup. A manicure. We have to double-check on the cake. And we should do something with your hair. Really, Hannah, it's bad enough to be doing this, but it would be a sin not to do it right."

Doing it right to me and doing it right to Ruby are two completely different things. I am much more concerned with how the whole nonwedding looked to people. She is much more concerned with how the nonbride looked to people.

"There's a lovely salon around the corner and we have appointments for, oh," Ruby says, stopping with her finger on her watch, "right now." She scoops my half-finished breakfast away from me, drops it in the sink, and disappears into the hall.

I sit there blankly and rub my fingers in the crumbs on the table. The butcher block needs to be treated again, and Drew was the only one who memorized the directions before I threw them away in a fit of cleaning last spring. I brush the crumbs away, running my fingers slowly over the soft nubs of wood that rise up unevenly on the table. The few sharp ones pierce my fingers, and I wince with pain but do not stop.

The kitchen door swings back in. I feel Ruby standing

behind me like a shadow. "Good thing you're dressed. Take a sweater."

She rests the sweater on the table next to me, but I don't move to put it on. I can't move. I feel stuck to that chair and that table, which will never be right again.

"Hannah, let's go. This will help."

"Help? Do you really think having a new hairdo will help?" I stand to face Ruby, leaving the sweater on the table. "I'll go, but please don't tell me it will help."

I start to feel a little wrong for my behavior as she follows ten steps behind me like some traditional concubine as we head up the street to La Femme Chic. After two blocks of feeling like I am being pursued by the FBI or some raging ex-boyfriend, I turn around and shout, "Come on already." She quickens her pace for a few feet, then settles into a slower gait. A very tall man dressed in a leather suit that is studded around the collar and the cuffs with bullet casings almost knocks her over. I watch a familiar look of indignation cross over my mother's face. "Excuse me," she says, running a little after the man, making three steps for each of his. "Sir, excuse me."

The studded man looks over his shoulder, and Ruby shoots a finger up at him, shaking it like a schoolmarm or elementary-school teaching nun. "Or should I say excuse you?"

"Fuck off, lady," he says, walking away while still

looking over his shoulder. The Chinese grocer wheels out a shopping cart filled over capacity with oranges into the sidewalk in front of him.

Ruby stops moving toward him and says, "You wait."

The studs along his collar take to the oranges on impact. He steps back from the cart with two navels stuck haphazardly to his lapel. We duck into La Femme Chic before he has a chance for rebuttal.

Ruby takes my hand as we settle down into the red velvet chairs in the waiting room. She is laughing uncontrollably, I think to myself, until I realize I am laughing uncontrollably. I will myself to stop.

"Hannah, it's okay to laugh when something's funny," Ruby says in a quiet whisper before flipping through a *McCall's* in the pile in front of us.

The idea that laughing is okay strikes me as wrong, 100 percent wrong. If I loved him, how could I be happy enough to laugh? But there are a whole lot of ifs involved. I close my eyes and try to picture Key West, our last vacation, pausing frame by frame over the moments I want to remember most, the times when I laughed, and it was okay because Drew was still laughing with me. Drops of moisture pool on my folded hands, and I know I must be crying, yet I am unable to open my eyes to check.

"Take a look," Ruby says as she pushes a hairstyle book onto my lap. It rests there until the hairdresser, a peppy brunette with red highlights and a green corduroy minijumper, takes it off.

"Who's going first?" she asks. I lift my head a little toward Ruby. This one is way too peppy for me.

"Lead by example," she says, disappearing into the shampoo area around the back.

With an open magazine on my lap, I settle my gaze on the street, content with the silence of waiting. I am the kind of person who likes to be in airports late at night waiting for a connection or in a diner after all the drunks have gone home. Those are the kind of places where pictures pop out at me, a photographer's dream. You catch so many things that are out of place or worn down after a long day's activity. And people are quieter, slower, and probably tired. Easier to take pictures of. I suddenly wish it was night, and that I had my camera. And that Ruby and my friends wouldn't follow me or find me. With my camera, I didn't have to make a sound.

This solitude is broken by an equally peppy blonde in a hot-pink corduroy minijumper. The only difference is that she has tights and boots to match. "Wanna get a wash before your cut?" she asks as if I had some kind of choice.

I stand up to indicate my answer and follow her hot-pink legs to the back.

"Have a seat," she says as she disappears around the bank of washbasins.

"I love this place," Ruby says to me as the peppy girl rests her head back into the sink. I am trying not to make a single sound. I close my eyes and relax into the washing girl's fingertips as she massages conditioner into my scalp.

The salon is nice enough, I suppose, has one of the best reputations in town, but the girl washing my hair can't stop talking about her collie. Not that I have anything against collies or Lassie or any other canine, just that Ruby's theory is beginning to soak in. I want to look good and not look like a collie. But how do you say that politely? So instead I just let her words about obedience training, halter leashes, and biscuits float over me, hoping she just washes hair and doesn't cut it, too. I don't think a Lassie cut would be befitting of a bride-not-to-be.

When I open my eyes, Ruby is gone. I hear her, though, discussing coloring options with some man who sounds a lot like Fox-Boy. I don't think he has a hand in this, so I let the thought go, until my stylist, Roberta Diem, complete with jet-black hair and black lipstick, appears to talk about my options.

"Okay," she says, in an accent I can't distinguish, something like one part Italian, one part North Jersey, one part New York, "You need something you can do yourself, the wedding is on Saturday right? So no up-do. We got perms, short cuts, and medium cuts. You have the book? No? Here, look at the book."

And she hands me a thick book with all the hairstyles she herself completed. Even though I am fighting it, I am impressed. The before and after shots are amazing, but I can't see my brown hair permed, dyed, or cut too short. I want an up-do. I file through those pages lingering on French braids and twists. Pastry hair-dos. Roberta stands by my chair and taps her foot on the hydraulic lever. "Saturday," she says. "No up-do."

I concede temporarily, out of respect for Ruby, who appears to be enjoying herself as the colorist pulls little sections of her hair and brushes them down on tinfoil dyed the color of red Kool-Aid. I hope it isn't Kool-Aid, some people did that now, and I never really wanted any member of my immediate family to become one of them. "Roberta," I say, "you pick. Lemme see the picture, then we'll talk."

She looks at me blankly.

"You are the professional."

A faint black-lipped smile breaks across her face as she scans through the pages of the book, coming to a medium cut that is a lot like a flip or something one of those anorexic girls on television wore.

"I know everyone has it, but I can shape it in around your face to make it less flippy, and if you want up-do," she says, catching the up-do tab, "you can do this with that cut." She points to a picture of the same girl with a great French braid, little tendrils lightly framing in her face.

"Perfect," I say, knowing it is, especially when Roberta starts and doesn't say a word. I respect her silence, and she respects mine. After twenty-nine years, I have finally found my hairdresser. Closing my eyes, my thoughts drift up out of the salon and back to Key West. I listen to the sounds of the waves crashing against the shore. Roberta taps my shoulder with the hair dryer to wake me up.

"Look," she says, spinning my chair around, handing me the mirror to see the back for myself.

I can't believe how long I was out of commission. Looking for Ruby, I find her under a dryer, rows of big pink curlers in her hair. She waves to me, not in the least alarmed at my new sleeping habits. She signals okay to me, beaming her proud smile. I know she likes to thank herself whenever I look halfway decent.

Roberta lets me sit there for a few minutes before leading me over to Bambi, the nail technician. "You okay?" she asks, setting me down in a chair like someone handling an elderly relation. "You sleep too long?"

I look down at my hands, which are shaky on the table. "Yeah," I say, "rough night."

"Yeah," she says, pointing to the dark circles under her eyes, "me, too."

I could really like that woman, I think as I watch her squeak herself and her combat boots across the floor, littered with little pieces of mine and everyone else's hair. Or would it be hairs? I didn't know, but the little chunks of it are scattered everywhere like something out of the MOMA. Someone could probably get away with that. Then again, some people can get away with everything or anything. I hope for an instant that I might be one of them Saturday. An anxious feeling wells up inside of me. Pastor Joe. The ceremony. Shoes. Bambi appears before the ulcer pains start to burn and growl. I could like her for that.

She is a pleasant-looking girl, trying too hard to be a Bambi, with the bleached hair and eyebrows, the maybe-plastic, maybe-Wonderbra chest, and the squeaky helium voice that escapes when she says, "Hi, how ya doin' today?"

I look in the mirror across from us on the wall. Despite my hair, which is in fact stellar and perfectly arranged, you can easily tell I am not doing very well. I decide not to lie. "Actually, Bambi, I'm a little nervous with this wedding on Saturday."

"Yeah, your mom said to do a French manicure because you're going to some wedding. Somebody you don't like?"

"No," I say, laughing, "it's my wedding."

"Oh, how funny your mother is. She didn't say that.

Well then, French manicure it is." Bambi laughs through her nose, sending chills up and down my spine. Mrs. Heinz laughed like that once, over Christmas dinner, the year after we got engaged. She had been laughing at me, at the fishing fly maker I bought for her husband. He'll never use that, she snorted out like a pig. Mr. Heinz smiled at me, thanked me profusely, adding that not a single word of Eleanor's was true. I wondered if that tenet was still in effect. And if she was a liar, would that lead to her attendance on Saturday for spite, even though she railed against the whole thing?

A new wave of anxiety washes through me. Bambi pushes my cuticle too hard. I begin counting the minutes until I can be at home on the couch, watching television mindlessly, wishing I had a cat to sit with me. Every proper spinster has a cat, I think, laughing a little to myself, trying to abate the sickness, failing miserably. Bambi scrapes the top of my fingers with the file, and then she begins to talk.

Normally, I don't mind the voices of strangers. In fact, when I take pictures, I like to know the stories behind people. But Bambi with her piggy laugh and the pain she is inflicting could become deaf and mute right this instant, and I do not feel the world would be missing a damn thing. I feel bad for thinking this, for feeling this way, and so I don't say anything to stop her as Bambi begins the story of her elopement.

"Well, I had this whole thing planned out with Anthony. The priest, the dress, the Manor on Route 9, fairy-tale stuff, a hundred and fifty dollars a head. Anthony's family was well-to-do, all right, they foot the bill for everything except my dress and the favors, my sister made both of them, but I didn't feel right about the whole thing. The priest was creepy, the food tacky, everything so like everyone else's. So I called Anthony one night, yeah, we had to stop sleeping together because of it," she says, stopping to shake the bottle of white polish for my tips, little bits of the plastic used to separate the two sections sticking to her hands, "and told him let's go down to Maryland, you and me, and get hitched, leave the big stuff behind. And get this, he said no. Oh, yeah, I said, and I called this guy Joe who I had been seeing until I got engaged, gave him the same pro-posal, and he said yes." She flashes the gold band and the huge diamond to me. "Tony's diamond," she adds, "he wanted this for the other tart that he found to say yes in time for all the plans his mother made, but I told him to shove off. If you couldn't marry a person when they asked, when could you?"

I don't want to listen to Bambi's sordid life anymore. I pray she would stick my fingers under the nail dryer and forget I exist. I yawn, and look beseechingly at Ruby, who is having her nails done by some nice woman from the Eastern bloc who doesn't appear to understand a word Ruby is saying. But Bambi doesn't move. "You done?" I ask.

"Yeah," she says, "but you have to dry fifteen minutes."

"Go take a break, you need one I'm sure."

"Really?" Bambi asks, picking herself up from the table.

"Go call Joe," I shout as she walks down the corridor to the back, relief spreading over me. I can't take much more of this. I want my life back. I want to sleep this bad dream off. I want to strangle Bambi and everyone of her kind. I want to strangle myself.

Ruby's nails take close to a half hour to dry, and by the third time Bambi comes over to offer me coffee, I leave my chair and return to the waiting area out of Bambi's patrol. Never underestimate yourself or your ability to fly off the handle. I flip through magazines just to hear the noise, eavesdrop on the receptionist's conversations with the owner about Bambi's shoddy work ethic, and try not to engage in any more conversations that might not turn out pleasant. I dart my eyes around a lot, avoiding eye contact with the older women, the weekly clients I guess, that fill the chairs around me waiting for their wash and sets. I pray I won't ever come to the salon once a week to have anything done let alone my hair. But that might be the proper widow thing to do. I opt to fly in the face of convention for that one, vowing to always find a way to wash my own hair.

Ruby finally appears with her hair and nails a new shade of red. She looks like a new woman, someone not my mother, someone not Allen's wife. I am proud of her looking good the same way she is proud of me, but I want to get out of that place, away from Bambi and Joe, and their magical ability to get married just because they could.

"So," Ruby says, "what's your pleasure for the afternoon? Shopping? Food?"

Drew used to meet me for lunch in one of his snappy suits, his tie blowing in the wind over his shoulder like a modern art sculpture. If only he could just be late. Late for lunch. Late for dinner. I would sink down to the curb and wait for him.

"So, what is it, Hannah?"

"Can we go home? I just really want to be home. I'm not—" I stop myself from telling her I didn't feel well, not wanting her to feel obligated to stay with me, almost not wanting her to stay. "Don't you need to check in on your place? With Allen gone and all, shouldn't you check messages?"

"Don't worry about me, I've got that under control. Remote answering system, and Allen has your number.

Let me stay with you, Hannah, I wouldn't if I didn't want to."

"What if I don't want you to?" I ask, regretting it almost instantly.

"I would pay you no attention. Hannah, just relax, I can see the stress in your face. Everything is going to be fine."

"Ruby, I would be stressed even in the best of circumstances. How can you stand there and expect me to be fine?"

Ruby stops walking and turns to face me, putting both her hands on my shoulders. "The worst is over. I know what it is like to lose the man you love long before you ever even conceived of the idea that he might not be there. You already know he's not away on business, out with his friends, or late coming home from work. You already know where Drew is and will be. The rest is inside you. Only you can take care of it. And only you know now what needs to be done, and if this Saturday will remedy your pain. So be it. And to hell with anyone who doesn't see it your way. Fuck them," she says.

I didn't realize my stress could be from worrying about what other people were going to say, but hearing her say it made sense. Fuck them. "No turning back," I say, wincing with the memory that I didn't call Pastor Joe today and that the ceremony remains unplanned.

"No turning back," she answers, sliding her one arm across my shoulders, guiding me into a pizza parlor for lunch. "You still like pizza?"

I nod, the smell of the pizzas in the oven touching me like a soft hand on my face. We are greeted heartily; Drew and I used to order a Sicilian with the works from here once a week.

"You starting early today? Regular order?" the man behind the counter, the one who called himself the Pizza Man in his cable television commercials, asks.

"No, no," I say quickly, not wanting to face a large Sicilian with the works. Stupid, I think, it's just pizza, but it is more than that. It was almost every major decision in our life. Whenever something big came up, we would sit around the apartment, discussing the damn thing to death until one of us finally broke down with *I'm hungry,* and the other would dial the Pizza Man. *Pizza Man to the rescue,* I would say, handing him the warm box, while I tried to open the door with our almost worn-out key. He would put his free hand on my back, gently pressing the warmth of him into me. *Relax,* he would say, *we'll figure it out, we always figure it out.*

To me, Drew was pizza. He was warm and filling, good at any time. He made many layers and could change toppings to suit the tastes of others, yet remain distinct and the same. He could be pineapple and ham one day, and familiar pepperoni the next. No matter what flavor, he was always available and good.

"Small with mushrooms, okay?" Ruby orders, looking at me and the Pizza Man. We both nod, and the Pizza Man sets himself to making a fresh one just for us. "Do you mind if we eat here? I'm afraid I didn't clean up from breakfast; no sense in adding to the mess."

"Fine." The smells of the place are overwhelming, as is the noise that comes in from the street every time someone opens the front door. A line begins to form behind the counter, women in suits with workout sneakers and men in ties hanging loosely around their necks. I look at my watch. Five-thirty. Drew's train would be pulling in at five fifty-two. If we sat here for twenty-five more minutes a month ago, Drew would walk past those windows. He would walk past those windows, and the shadow to the words Pizza Man cut out of the awning would shimmer over his body in a special effect that I would photograph and hang on the wall with all my other memories of him. After the picture was hung on the wall, I would go into the kitchen and find him again, pizza on his plate in front of him, smell the Old Spice on his neck, kiss him, and tell him that I really was glad he was going to be my husband for the rest of all time.

The Pizza Man produces in grand style one small pizza

with mushrooms, kissing Ruby on the cheek. "Welcome," he says before she has a chance to say thank you.

She gently taps her wedding ring against the table, batting her eyelashes at him.

"You bring your husband next time," he says, bowing backwards behind the counter. "He could sit in back with my wife."

"What a lovely place!"

"You just like Hoboken, don't you? Shame Allen's not an engineer. Stevens is two blocks from here."

"Don't tease. We both know Allen wouldn't leave Princeton or that house or anything."

Allen comes to mind for a minute, the pictures of his missing kids, the way my mother's things seemed tucked in around his. "No, Ruby, I don't know Allen."

"What do you mean? You've met him, taken meals with him. What don't you know?"

I pause, trying to think if what I am going to say would come out wrong. My mother's husband is always a touchy subject. One of her biggest fears is that we wouldn't like each other. Ruby wants everyone in her life to get along. "I like him, you know, he seems very nice. But I just don't know him. Like leaving the house. I thought he didn't leave it because, oh, I don't know. I just didn't know he liked it."

"Oh, but it's not that you don't like him, is it? I'm

sure if he's ever done anything to offend you it wasn't on purpose. He is a very thoughtful man."

"No, no. I just don't know him, that's all. Like what to get him for his birthday. His favorite colors or books he likes to read. That kind of thing."

"Well, I can tell you anything about him."

"But it's not just him," I say. "I don't know a lot of people, come to think about it."

Ruby stops eating to listen to me. Thoughts are firing rapidly all over my mind. "My father or Louis or Drew even. I never take the time to remember. Maybe I never realized I would have to remember. I guess I just always thought they were going to be there."

"You were too little to remember your father. And Louis left us on the first bus out of town. You can't be expected to know everything."

"But what about him?" I ask.

"Eat," she says. "Don't beat yourself up about this. You'll remember, Hannah, so much that you'll want to forget."

I could see by her eyes that she was thinking of my father and Louis, the great loves and losses of her life. I wonder how she looks at Allen when he flies off to conferences on the Third World in the Third World. Does she worry that he's not ever coming back? That some danger may rip him from her like it took my father. Or that another woman could lure him away. Does she ever stop worrying that he'll leave, that everyone will leave?

We continue our meal in silence despite Ruby's several valiant attempts to change the subject. I know why I didn't take the time, I tell the Ruby in my head, because I never expected anyone to stay. By the time we get back to the apartment, it is dark, except for the answering machine, which blinks one new message. I cover its light with the wedding pamphlet and turn on the television with the remote. Ruby and I sit in the glow of the television, mesmerized by the sitcoms and medical dramas. I finally feel my body fall away, leaving me heavy and light at the same time, deep into an unsound sleep, uncovered and exposed on the couch. Thoughts of all else slip away from me, and I am glad. Enough is enough.

Monday, November 13, 1995

Brake lights arc and shimmer in the few fat drops of rain on my windshield. The wipers scrape dry for a few passes. Drew reaches over and turns them off.

"This rain reminds me of that movie we saw last week. The one with the woman, with the tire in the rain. Creepy, you know."

"Don't get weirded out or anything, you're not alone," he says, switching the wipers back on.

I signal to turn into the mainly empty mall parking lot. "I'm not weirded out, I was just thinking."

"You think too much," he says, pausing to draw in a deep breath. Pausing like he's been holding something in for a long time and finally needs to get it out. "Lemme rephrase that, you think too much about stuff that doesn't matter. The stuff that doesn't effect you. Too much, H, way too much."

Too much, I say under my breath, not wanting to start something. "Whatever," I say, taking in my own deep breath. "I just meant the way everything looked in the rain."

"Yeah," Drew says, "it is kind of creepy how all the lights seem to flare up at you."

He picks up my hand as we swish through the automatic doors. Inside, the whole film noir effect kicks back in, like an episode of the *Twilight Zone*. Even though this is our mall, as in where we make and have made all our major purchases for the last three years, I am taken aback by the disparate pairs of men and women milling around in duck boots and polar fleece. Their hair is wet and matted down to their skulls. They look at the store windows and not each other, moving as if by radar, without colliding into their partner or other couples. It's Monday Date Night at the movies, buy one, get one free, and only the consummate dating couples are out. They are done trying to impress each other, and they sure as hell aren't trying to impress anyone else.

I look down at Drew's Doc Martens.

I untoggle the drawstring of my polar fleece pullover.

I try not to think about it, pointing out instead to Drew a couple our age, lip-locked in front of the record

store. I notice her engagement ring the size of Tucson
and decide not to point that out. Drew's grandmother's
is two times the size of it. He has offered it to me twice
before, once eight months after we met and once again
after he moved in last year. If he runs on a schedule, he is
due to ask again in the fall. The thought makes my stomach flip in a sort of queasy excitement and fear. Being
married would change everything. Being married would
change me. I think about my mother, one of the few
married women I know, and shudder at the thought of
ever giving myself up so completely.

He casually ignores them as we pass, raising his eyebrows at me for a moment. "Big crowd," he says, refer-
ring to the movie-theater line ahead. "You have to
admire the power of the buy one, get one on a rainy
Monday night. If Jesus used this instead of miracles, he
would have drawn a bigger crowd."

"And *I* think too much," I say. "Since when did you
become religious?"

"Since when did saying Jesus out loud in a public
place make you religious? God."

"There you go again. I thought you were awfully
interested in that Bible at the Holiday Inn in Florida." I
place my hand on his stomach and tickle him through
the space between the buttons on his flannel shirt.

He kisses my hand, and I can't help but think about

the pope, but that would be me kissing his hand. Or the gross couple in front of the record store. I pull my hand away from his and put it safely away in my pocket.

In line for the movie, I kind of stand behind him, let him scan the posters and the times, watch where his eyes linger the longest. Provided that the film doesn't star Steven Seagal, Jim Carrey, or any woman who would answer if someone shouted playmate, I'll go with his choices. He's usually not that far from the mark. Heck, he cried at *Forrest Gump*. Not even his mom cried at *Forrest Gump*.

"Is it going to be a long one?" I ask.

The line moves forward in increments of two. The polar-fleeced, duck-booted couples walk off separately to find popcorn and the best seats in the theater. I try to figure out which man goes with which woman as they team back up. It's like doing a puzzle, only the pieces move by themselves. I wonder if I was a puzzle piece, if Drew would be the piece next to me. Or if the person doing the puzzle would even see fit to put us together in the first place.

"Does it matter? I thought you said it didn't matter." His brow furrows a little in panic; the choice was obviously a long one.

"Drew, I just wanted to know if I should pee now or later, if you really have to know every detail."

"*Braveheart,* okay?" he asks.

"Yeah," I say, as if I ever say no. "Meet me by the water fountain."

I walk away with a bit of a strut, knowing that even after three years, he still watches me. His eyes catch mine as I round the corner. He waves, like a three-year-old child, or maybe a father.

The rest room before the movie is always empty. You would think people would see fit to pee before they sit down in a six-dollar-and-seventy-five-cent seat and drink a half gallon of soda they paid close to five additional bucks for—but no—they wait until the movie gets to the good part. Then they worm past you to get out, your knees bunched into your chin, your own bladder now squashed, and only after you've regained feeling in your lower back, they return, and proceed to whisper, *What did I miss, what, he what, oh I can't believe I missed that.* In this case, I pee first and ask Drew if we can sit away from people.

Public bathrooms always amaze me. Especially when they are different from what you would expect. Like the ones at fancy restaurants in the city. I've been in some of the nastiest bathrooms at the nicest places. But movie theaters, despite the throngs of soda-drinking, popcorn-eating machines, are the cleanest I've seen with one exception.

I-love-Marcos-4-Ever is scrawled in red Magic Marker across the door to my stall, along with a slew of other endearing expressions of love and undying passion. *I-*

screwed-Marcos-4-Hours is written farther down on the list, in a markedly different handwriting. I try to imagine myself professing undying love to Drew Heinz with a Magic Marker in the bathroom of the Route 1 General Cinemas. What's the point if I know JE Loves KL or that Marcos gets around? People amaze me.

So do the automatic flusher and the automatic faucets. Now all they need are automatic doors to get out for the completely germ–free exit. With my hands under the lukewarm water, I try not to stare at the girl penciling her eyes with black liquid eyeliner. I wonder if she knew Marcos. She shoots me a look that says stop staring or I'll poke your eyes out. Her platform shoes clack against the tile floor as she steps back to survey her pierced belly button, which peaks over the top of her skintight Adidas running pants, zippers opened at the ankles, flaring over the shoes. Another girl in a matching outfit only in reverse, white shoes, white pants, black Adidas stripes, steps out the stall behind me. I wipe my hands on my pants, quickly exiting.

Drew is waiting for me by the water fountain, eyeing up the popcorn a short boy in overalls is shoving into his mouth. When Drew was a senior in high school, he saved a boy's life by performing the Heimlich in the lunchroom. The guy still calls Drew every once in a while, and we even went to his wedding. The first time Drew proposed was after that wedding. I told him to think about it and ask me again when the champagne wore off. And he did, two years later, to which I replied, "Maybe later." He shrugged and said, "Your loss." But he didn't leave or move out or even bring it up again. Not that I wanted him to or anything, just that he didn't.

"Hey," I say.

"Hey," he says, squeezing my hand while checking the popcorn boy out over my shoulder.

"He'll be okay," I tell him, squeezing his hand back, wondering if it's even something he thinks about, or if it's just me thinking about it.

The gross couple saunters past us, barely looking up in between wet tongue kisses to see where they are going. She giggles, "Stop it, Mark," as he pinches her butt. I think about the graffiti and start to laugh a little to myself. Drew looks at me funny, shaking his head.

"You know, Drew, I was thinking, and I just don't feel right about us seeing each other anymore. I was in the bathroom and—"

He drops my hand and steps in front of me. "Why are you doing this?"

And I look at him for a minute before figuring out what to say. I never expected him to take this so seriously. I was only joking. "Wait, it's not what you think, I was just in the bathroom and—"

"And what, you don't want to be with me anymore? See something better in there?"

"Drew, could you just relax a minute, it's just that all these girls have written all over the stalls, things like *I love Fred forever. Michael is Mine Today, Tomorrow, and Always.* You know, and I just didn't feel compelled to put pen to wall, so to speak."

"So because we're not thirteen and hanging out at the mall, you don't love me anymore."

He starts walking toward the theater. He pulls open the door and steps inside without holding it open for me. I catch it with the tips of my fingers, bending my pinkie nail back.

"Could you just listen to me," I whisper to him. "I was only joking."

"That's really not funny," he says.

"Come on, it wouldn't matter if I did write our names on the wall. It's not like anyone I know comes here. And how does anyone know the Jennifer K. that loves Michael means the same Jennifer K. that sits across from them in business math?"

"If you had a unique name, people would know, don't you think, Hannah?" Drew smiles, thinking he has won a point.

"Yeah, but how many people do we know that come here?" I turn to face the screen. *Who was the first actor to be kissed in a color movie?* slides across the screen.

"Toto, the dog?" I ask.

"My mother," he says.

"I know she got around, but your mother was not in *The Wizard of Oz*."

"No, not the trivia question. My mother comes here all the time."

I thought about his mother for a minute, and she could have been in the movie. Maybe one of the lollipop kids. A winged monkey. I thought about her in the bathroom, chatting with the stranger next to her about her sciatica and the pinch of the movie seats on her back. I could almost hear her suck in her breath, seeing her son's name written in a bathroom stall next to mine. Even after we moved to Hoboken together, she never gave up hope that it was all some big mistake.

"Give me a pen," I say, standing up and smoothing down the wrinkles in my jeans. "Be right back."

"H, don't be stupid," he says.

"I wasn't being stupid; you're the one that brought it up." I lift my purse to my lap and begin digging through it in search of a pen. It is suddenly very important to me to write on that wall.

"No, you're the one that started the whole thing by breaking up with me."

Ink from a leaking purple pen dots my hand as I wave the pen triumphantly in front of him. "I was just having fun. Come on, wouldn't it be fun—"

"To break up, yeah H, loads of fun. Watch the damn previews."

"Let me finish what I was saying. Wouldn't it be fun to see if your mother found out that Hannah loves Drew forever?"

"Wouldn't that be some sort of commitment? An engagement maybe?" He grabs the pen by the cap. The heat of his hand warms mine. The ink flows sticky between our fingers.

I let go of the pen and watch it fall from his hand to the floor. It rolls a few inches and stops against a discarded box of popcorn. The theater darkens, and Drew turns toward the screen. The outline of Drew's face glows in the bright lights from the bomb-scare movie preview that explodes across the screen. He puts his hand on my knee, offers me some of his soda. He turns to look at me, the cool soda touching my arm, shivers up and down my spine.

Friday, October 24, 1997

This was supposed to be a different day entirely. I was supposed to wake up and have my hair done. Be too nervous to eat. Make lots of phone calls. Double-check the flowers and the cake. Try on my dress. Watch everyone else try on their dresses. Drink a little too much. Drink a little more. Maybe see a stripper. A good-looking stripper. Smile like a fool. Smoke a cigarette to calm my nerves. Brush my teeth with a whitening toothpaste. Sleep on my back so as not to ruin the facial or the moisturizing cream. Have happy, nervous dreams of running away with the man I love, the man who will be my husband. Wake up the next day smiling. Smile the whole day. Be kissed by Drew a thousand times before dinner. The day before the happiest day of my life. Instead, I can't bear to move, not even to shield my eyes from the sunbeam that is blinding me in my place. Instead, I close my eyes and try to sleep more. To return to the dream I had, the dream that was supposed to be today. The dream that was supposed to be my life.

This fight between asleep and awake continues on until after noon with Ruby trying to referee. A referee on the side of sunshine and the alarm clock ticking away the day. She tries everything. Making coffee from the gourmet store, the aroma filtering through the air of the apartment like expensive women's perfume. Frying hash browns and pancakes. Letting the phone ring five times without answering. Talking loudly to the people who did call about me and Drew and the wedding. She opens and shuts the door to my room at least five times an hour, asking me each time if I need anything. By the twelfth time, I give in. "Coffee," I shout. "I'd like some coffee if it would make you happy."

"The only thing that would make me happy now is for you to be happy. Or at least up out of bed. It is one o'clock in the afternoon. And Joe called again, he'll be here in forty-five minutes."

I stare at the ceiling above my bed for what feels like five minutes. In forty minutes, I will have to decide on a wedding to a man who is no longer alive. What would Drew say about that? Strong stockbroker Drew, crier at weddings and Hallmark commercials. What would he say if he was next to me right now? Would he lean up on his side, his hand holding up his head, and look quizzically at me, like a puppy trying to understand human voices? Would I kiss his knuckles nested in his springy brown curls? Would he ask me why? Or would he just nod and say *all right* like some hippie caught in a groove? Would he say he loved me? That he understood? Would he kiss me on the nose like he used to when we first started dating, and he was afraid to kiss me on the lips in public? Would he sympathize, say he would do the same if he was in my shoes? *What should I do?* I'd ask, leaning on my own side, hand holding up my head. Drew would put his free hand behind my neck and roll his fingers over my spine like he was playing slow scales on a piano. Goose pimples would spring up on my arms, and as he leaned in to kiss me, he'd say, *Up to you, H,* the one thing I could always count on him saying; it was a close second to him saying *I love you.*

A familiar headache throbs behind my eyes. There is no use in saying if only it hadn't been left up to me for so long. If only he'd put his foot down, just once, and said, *Enough already, we're getting married.* Instead, I never had to think about, mull over ceremonies or processionals, and now, I can't even imagine what it could be like. My mind draws a blank. I sit up straight in the bed and tug at the shade through the brass bars of the headboard. More sunlight washes over the white blankets and glints off the footboard. I used to think that Drew's eyes would capture the candlelight at our wedding ceremony, and that there would be candles. And that his hands wouldn't even be sweaty, but that mine were. That it would go quickly, and he'd be my husband, no matter what, until death do us part.

Ruby walks in with my coffee and sets it on the nightstand. "I don't care if you don't change into some clothes, but you might want to."

I don't answer her because I don't have an answer for her. I pick up the coffee mug and hold it with both hands, feeling suddenly cold. "Until death do us part," I say to myself.

"Yeah, bummer, definitely should not include that tomorrow."

"What? We have to serve coffee, people expect coffee with cake."

"No, the until death do us part, ask Joe to cut that out. I'm sure he has ideas though. Very capable man. Good-looking, too."

"Ruby, I am not in the market for a good-looking man. How can you even say that?"

She smoothes the duvet next to me and sits down. "Really, I meant for the aesthetics of the day. Drew spent all that money on flowers, why would you want some troll of a minister standing in the middle of white roses?"

"Oh," I say, guilty for not realizing there could be

another meaning to Ruby's comment. How could I think that? I decide not to change, to not make any kind of effort to seem presentable. I wouldn't want anything to be taken the wrong way by me, him, or Ruby. Guilt weighs down on me, turning my empty stomach in circles. "Do we have any bagels?"

"No, but I could go."

"Really?" I ask, still amazed that Ruby is here and doing things for me. Selfless things. Random acts of kindness. I look at her for a few minutes, straining to see if this woman could somehow not be the Ruby I grew up with. The woman who used to look past me in the morning, in order to see into the eyes of the man she just woke up with. Or the woman who rushed out of my thesis showing to get to a hair appointment. That day, she blew through the university gallery stopping at two pictures, one of which wasn't even mine, gave me a double kiss on each cheek, and then left like some kind of tornado. Where is my mother?

She stands, repositions her black skirt over her knees. I watch her walk from the room. "Hannah," she calls out from the living room, "don't worry, I really don't mind helping. I honest."

The sound of her words turns over in my mind. Honest. I would have never thought my mother's feelings for me were honest. Honest implies up-front, straightforward, and I guess for the first time, she is as she seems.

Ruby is both my mother and someone's wife. For the first time in that order. The alarm clock on my night table shoots off a traffic report for no reason, and I realize that I only have twenty minutes until Joe will be there. I decide to brush my teeth, but not change.

I stumble into the bathroom without turning on the light. I put toothpaste on the toothbrush, run it under some water, and manage to only lose a little toothpaste down the drain. I absentmindedly brush in circles, twirling my hair around a finger on my free hand, the fresh-cut ends of it feeling alien, like the hair from a doll. I start on my molars, brushing hard, and getting no strength. I take the toothbrush out of my mouth to inspect the bristles. It is Drew's. I drop it in the sink, rinse my mouth, and leave the bathroom uncomfortable with the thought that what was his is losing its identity, that it will all become mine and slowly disappear into the ooze of life as it goes by.

Things like this start small, and soon enough, I'll be cutting his shirts into rags, using his shoes as doorstops, sleeping in the middle of the bed. I look all around at the apartment: his briefcase, his favorite mug, the desk filled with countless tax-deductible receipts. I think about all the things that will be, or have already been shoved aside, boxed up, or given away. How all the things that meant something to him, that were a part of his life, could disappear much the same way Drew did. And that I will let it happen. I sink into the couch, careful to sit in the spot that was mine on the right-hand side and wait for Ruby to come back.

There is slight knock on the door, so I say *come in,* expecting Ruby, bags of bagels, flavored cream cheese. Instead, Joe walks in, Pastor Joe, complete with collar and a *Father Knows Best* gray sweater. But the sweater hangs on him funny, a little too large and droopy; it's like even the sweater knows this man belongs in jeans and a T-shirt. As he steps inside and turns to shut the door behind him, I think about the field day Fox-Boy would have dressing as a man of the cloth. The thought amuses me so much that I chuckle out loud.

"Well, well, well, you're feeling better. Great," he says, truly pleased by this thought.

"Yes and no. Depends on the moment." He sits down near my feet, which I quickly sweep under me. My pajama bottoms stretch thin over my knees where the flannel has worn away with too many washings and wearings. I run my finger over the smooth, thin patches, not wanting to look up.

This doesn't stop him from continuing. He leans forward slightly, trying to catch my eyes with his gaze. "To tell you the truth, I wasn't sure what I would find or if I was even welcome. I put some research into this and came up with a few things that I'd really like you to take a look at. There's several poems and a few different ways we could run the ceremony. Okay?"

"You're welcome," I say.

"I'm glad, but is it okay?"

"Okay?"

Joe rests his arm on the side of the couch and extends a folder toward me. "The ceremony and the poems, is that okay?"

"Poems and ceremony," I repeat stumbling over my words. "Yes, okay, that's why you're here, right?"

"Yes, of course," he says, the wrinkles disappearing from his forehead. "Let's begin with the ceremony. What are your thoughts?"

His grins an eager smile at me, his cheeks bunched under his eyes, which are bright, burning bright with enthusiasm. To explain to him that I have no thoughts would be just as hard as explaining to everyone Drew ever knew why we didn't get married a long time ago. How can I convince a man who believes you can turn some matzo and grape juice into the body and blood of Christ that if I even visualize something for one moment, believe in it, or want it, that it will disappear like a rabbit in a magician's hat? I smile weakly back at him, a half-smile, half-frown. I finger the crusty sleep left in the corner of my right eye and stare at the grain of the wood floor behind the couch.

"Well then, I start. Do you have that pamphlet I gave you? No, okay, here's another." He hands me a duplicate of the one I have in the other room. "Thanks be unto God for his unspeakable gift" from 2 Corinthians 9:15 is in small script across the bottom.

"Unspeakable," I say, taking heart in the thought that even good Christians have some things they'd rather not speak of.

"Okay, let's work on the traditional form, it starts on the inside cover." He reaches over my lap to open the book. His knuckles are bony and white, hairless. He points to the section titled Minister Speaks. "You've heard this before. Miracle of Love, God's union, special gifts."

I nod, unsure of the right answer.

"Yes, good. But is that something you are okay with? I might put a little spin on it, to calm the relations. Something like even though Drew no longer walks the physical earth, Hannah wanted to make one last proclamation before you, him, and God as a testament to their love. How's that?"

I feel his voice switching back into the used-car salesman tone he had in his office. I wonder if it is part of his job or if he has something at stake here. "What's the deal?" I ask.

"Deal?" He points to his chest as if to say, who me?

"Yeah, why are you so willing to do all of this? What

is the deal?" I push my back against the arm of the couch, letting its wood frame press in between my vertebrae. I bring my knees up under my chin and watch him, waiting for a response.

"Listen," he starts, his voice returning to the minister lull, "grief management is my kind of work. I do mainly hospice with AIDS patients and many of them never came to terms with their loved ones while they were alive. You know, the whole 'My family won't accept me because I'm gay,' or because 'I used drugs,' or because 'I'm sick.' People and their families get real torn up, and then when they pass away, there's nothing left. I was hoping that I could see how this ritual gets you through. See if it helps, so maybe it could help others in—don't take this the wrong way—worse situations."

"Worse?" I ask, offended even though he asked me not to be.

"Yeah, come on, Hannah, if you were a gay man and Drew, the man you were going to marry, died, do you really think your mother would be in the kitchen making coffee and taking your phone calls?"

I let his point float in the air between us. He was right; things could be worse. "Yeah," I say, "your wording's okay. I trust you with it."

"Good, good, good." Joe reaches his hand out toward me. "Really, it will be fine," he says, squeezing my fingers. "I do think we should leave out the vows though."

"Till death do us part."

"Yeah, especially that one, okay?"

"Yeah," I say, "okay."

Ruby storms in the door with an even bigger bag of bagels than I expected. "Just couldn't decide," she says, floating past us into the kitchen, the warm smell of the bagels hanging in the air like a trail.

"Want some?" I ask.

"No, let's get this nailed down. After I say the part about your testament, I think you should say something or read one of these. Something to get your feelings out into the open." He flips open another folder and pulls out a few sheets of cream-colored paper. Poems shine off the page in a glossy black ink.

"Thanks," I say, putting them on the coffee table. "Lemme think about that."

"Fine, but after you read I'd like to say a little blessing and close the whole thing up." Pastor Joe closes his manila folder and slips it into his backpack. "Must go."

His abrupt announcement surprises me, and I am at once glad and confused by his departure. I thought he wanted to get this nailed down. "You sure you don't need to know what I'm going to say? You don't want a bagel?"

"Nah, I trust that whatever you have to say is between you and him. If it's something you want to do, you'll work it out." He offers his hand once again to shake good-bye. "See you tomorrow, Ruby," he calls out, heading toward the door.

"Oh, see ya, Joe," Ruby answers, stepping out of the kitchen, drying her hands on a dish towel, like a mother from a fifties television program. "How'd that go?"

"Okay, I guess." I step past her and down the hallway to the bedroom. I pick a pair of jeans off the floor and trade them for my pajama bottoms. I put a sweater over my pajama top and slip on little sneakers from under the bed. In the living room, I grab the poems from the coffee table, and head for the door. "I gotta run some errands," I tell Ruby as I walk out. As I turn my key in the lock, I hear her call out to me about bagels. I keep moving down the hall to the stairs.

A light breeze blows through the main street. The hair of people walking in the opposite direction of the wind billows in front of them like it's some kind of new hairstyle or their hair is in a race with their head to get to the Path Station first. I turn into the wind and let the cool pulses push against me. I fight them and make my way up the street.

Stopping at a pay phone, I dial Fox-Boy's office number. He answers in a singsong voice that lets everyone know it is not his job to answer phone calls from the general public.

"Hello, hello, back at you," I say, "how about you

and Rena come over tonight, bring any munchies or mud masks and stay up with me? Paint our toenails?"

"Hannah, you know I don't do that."

"Do what? Paint your toenails? That is an out-and-out lie. I have seen those toes just about every shade of the rainbow. Don't even try to fool me."

"No, eat junk food and get a facial. Too much oil on chips."

"Fine, I'll slice up some carrot sticks. Okay?"

"Yeah, okay. Whaddaya think, I'm going to say no, no, no?"

"I'll see you after work," I say, hanging up the phone.

I begin to wander aimlessly, stopping at different shops to look in the windows, knowing I still need shoes, really jazzy shoes that make little tapping sounds when you walk.

This desire, this noise in my head, draws me into the first shoe store I find. Not that you would normally notice it is a shoe store. The shoe store is done in a style that tried to hide the fact that it is indeed a store. Understated windows with teak trim and a little sign in the lower-right-hand corner of the door that reads ALISTAR— THE SHOES make up the facade. Inside, the ceiling soars to about twenty feet, and a fake sky scene is painted on the ceiling. The try-on benches are made of a curved teak. Backless so that you can barely sit on them without feeling off kilter. The lighting is directed up from the polished stone floor in the fashion of landscape lighting. Two ficus trees dominate the front of the store, framing either side of the main shoe display table. White lights hang in the recesses of their boughs. The open-slat style of shelves that line the walls also match the benches, letting the lighting shoot through and surround each shoe without shadows. I step cautiously toward the rack of shoes, unsure if I am about to be asked to play Frisbee in this indoor park or for my credit card.

For all the mimicry of an earthy park, the shoes are mighty impractical, not a single flat to be found. Thin heels of six-inch stilettos in every pastel shade balance on the thin wood slats and easily tip over whenever I reach for a pair. It is so obvious that the high heels would fall over on such a system that it was most likely that this was done on purpose, either to keep the clerks busy, to record which shoes get noticed, or drive everyone involved crazy. After I demolish three racks of evening sandals, the sales clerk, in a long flowing mint-green pastel skirt with matching tailored jacket, proudly offers me assistance. The scarf around her neck picks up the faint rose pattern on her skirt. Her hair falls into a perfect upturned bob.

"Is there something in particular I could help you with?" she asks, as though my answer might be something other than a pair of shoes.

I try to explain the dress, the color, the chiffon, the

swirling skirt. "It's so funny, when I put it on, I heard high heels on a dance floor. I was hoping for something to match the skirt. And make that noise."

"Noise," she says, clearing her throat, bringing a small hand to the scarf around her neck. A small diamond ring barely glitters on her left hand, and her fingernail polish is chipping at the cuticles. "With a tea-length skirt you can go as high as you like, but for balance you might want to stay under three inches. Did you see any styles you liked? If you like we can take your measurements and then pull the specifications you're looking for?"

"Specifications?" I ask.

"Well, yes," she says, hand back on throat, "these are custom-made shoes. We send out orders daily to Italy and France depending on the type of leather or fabric requested. We can even do beading to match a specific dress."

"Oh," I say, quite unable to say anything else. "Thanks, I'll think about it and come back."

Immediately relief takes over when I am back on the street in my own domain, feeling very sluggish. Not wanting to give up and go home, I duck into the first coffeeshop I see, remembering I only had one cup this morning and nothing to eat.

The whole place smells like coffee; they could fry one thousand eggs, bake fifty apple and spice pies, roast a pig maybe, and you still wouldn't smell it over the Kenya

AA or the Vanilla Hazelnut. You could get high on the
fumes in this place, and for a few minutes I am giddy like
a child in Grandma's kitchen as the cookies come out of
the oven. I order a grande café latte with whipped cream
and a shot of caramel. The sugar and the caffeine should
help. Help with what, though? I ask myself.

Sitting there watching the people pass on the street,
some with dogs, many with briefcases, a few with those
three-wheeled off-roading baby carriages, I realize the
hardest part of this is not being able to see what will
become of all of this. Where will it go from here? The
people pass by and quite a few stop in. They know each
other. A woman in a floor-length faux fur steps up to
order coffee for her office. Her coiffed hair matches the
fur, highlight for highlight. Sunglasses cover half her
face.

"I thought I said large," she says. "Ah, hell, just dump
that into a big cup, it's for Marcy, she'll never know."

A woman with a broken arm comes up from the back
of the store and taps her on the shoulder. "Renee, I love
the hair. Great color. I didn't even recognize it was you."

"Steven, oh, look, yes, there he is, Steven did it for
me last week."

A man who is apparently Steven the Hairdresser walks
in and exchanges bourgeois cheek kisses with both
women.

"Great job the other night. You read so well," says the

broken-arm woman, waving her finger at Steven the Hairdresser. "I don't normally like poetry, but you were fabulous. Let me get you a coffee."

"Thank you, thank you," he says in a tone of a man used to accepting gifts from women admirers.

And it goes on like this with more people coming in and going out. Steven the Poet-Hairdresser seems to know everyone well enough to wave to quite a few of them. It's like a great big web spreads out from him and connects all these people together. I wish I had my own acquaintance web, one as big as Steven's. Drew used to say that about Hoboken, about how after seeing a few people over and over again like on the train or in the bodegas, you got to know them, maybe not their name but stuff about them, how they lived, the stuff that was on their minds.

"You talk to strangers about us?" I asked him with complete disbelief as he explained the local social system.

"It's like going to a shrink, you get stuff off your mind, make a little conversation, go away feeling a lot better about things. Strangers can do amazing things for a person," he said.

I wish I could be like that now. I wish I could say to the lady making espresso, "Boyfriend passed away, having the wedding anyway. What are you going to do?" and have her nod, ask me if I want another latte or perhaps a biscotti. I think about Joe, the one stranger I have said that to. I feel in my pocket for the poems he gave me. Pulling them out, I flip them over and take out a pen. I want to try writing my own before I cop out and use his. Drew was the man I loved, and I should have something to say about that. I should.

I put his name at the top of the page as if I am writing a letter to him. Drew. A list of adjectives and nouns fly through my head. *Best friend. Boyfriend. Generous. Loving. Kind. Hopeful. Happy.* But it all sounds like a eulogy. Something you say about the dead and not to them. I start again: *Drew, you were my past, my present, and my future, and no matter how hard I fought it . . .* My thoughts stop there, filled with embarrassment of only photographing my engagement ring, of only photographing Drew, of only living behind my camera and my fears and not in the real world. I used to think that behind my camera I was safe. The film put a layer between me and everything and everyone else. I control everything that crossed the frame of my camera's lens. Even my emotions. At least that's what I thought.

I start over: *Drew, I was so caught up in keeping everything the same I forgot to enjoy the many ways that things change. I'm sorry, and I'm here today, however too late, to tell you that I did and still would marry you and be with you as your partner.*

I lean back in my chair and smile, having finally found my words.

I finish my latte, still hungry, but I decide to keep going. Shoes are my new objective, my mission. Shoes that aren't custom-made or quiet on wood floors. Dancing shoes. It is silly, but when I put on that dress, I could hear tapping feet. I could hear me, walking across that parquet reception floor, turning to face the crowd, turning to face myself. I hear the words I wrote explaining, proclaiming, making things better.

I walk six more blocks, and my desperation grows. The breeze gets cooler, and the sun starts lowering itself in the sky. Across the street the orange PAY NO SUCH PRICE SHOE STORE sign glows like a beacon in the river. As I push through the door, I start making up the excuse I would need to tell Ruby the Shopping Queen about why I bought off-price, knockoff shoes. It isn't that the shoes didn't look nice; they did, knockoff cheap copies of designer styles. *Quality,* both the real-life Ruby and the Ruby-in-my-mind remind me, *is worth something and usually that means more money*. It is her one economic theory, and she is proud of it. Pay No Such Price runs against all of her traditions, cuts to her marrow, you could say. I walk to the aisle allocated for my size, surprisingly finding several pairs of cream- and white-colored shoes, all a little strappy, all perfect with pale yellow chiffon.

"Summer clearance," the counter girl shouts back at me, snapping her gum wildly between her braced teeth. "Seventy percent off."

I pull boxes off the shelf, precariously balancing them on the vinyl-upholstered bench alongside me. The smoothness of their fake silk, the way it slides under my fingers, how light it is, appeals to me. I slip the first pair on and am immediately disappointed. The store is carpeted. I look at the three boxes next to me and decide to buy them all.

"Special occasions," the counter girl says, pointing at me.

"Yeah," I say. "A wedding. My wedding." I stumble over the words in a botched effort to assert them, embarrassed that she asked, embarrassed that Drew was right about people asking.

"No, the shoes, eighty percent off."

I turn around to find an end cap of bright white shoes of all styles, with glittery, beaded stickers you can attach to them to spice them up a bit.

"Dyeable, see." The gum girl points to a row of pastel jars of liquid dye. Dye It! is written in wild script across the clear plastic. Little cotton-ball applicators float in the middle like some specimen saved for further examination.

"You brush on more and more coats to get the match. Easy."

I locate my size in the highest heel, abstaining from the beaded shoe stickers, finding the two shades of yellow dye they carry. I buy this along with the others, confident that Ruby would decide which is better. Make that hoping Ruby would not notice the Pay No Such Price bag and boxes. Maybe I am losing it. Maybe I shouldn't care about the bag or boxes or losing it. Maybe it is time I just live, became a part of the rest of the world, put things on the line. Live my own life, not just a life. Carpe diem and seize the shoes.

I guess the only part about getting home after dark by myself that bothers me is my street. With one streetlight at the beginning and the other blown out at the end, you walk through a flood of light into a pool of darkness. I always fumble with my keys to the front door, misstep the front steps. The hallway light is also burned out. So when I finally make it in, I feel my way along the wall to the door to the stairs. At least they are lighted, but by that time the damage was already done, I am hyped up from being alone and disoriented in the dark. I jog up the stairs and burst into my apartment completely out of breath, not expecting to find Rena, Fox-Boy, Miranda, and Ruby.

"Surprise," they shout, raising their arms up like a Broadway cast. It makes me smile. They make me smile.

Ruby steps forward first. "Listen, if you don't want to do this you don't have to. If you don't feel like it, just say so."

"No, it's fine. Totally fine," I say. "Wait, it's more

than fine, it's great. I just hope you remembered the beer."

"We have something better than beer," Rena says, putting her arm around me, leading me to the buffet table covered in junk food. "Ruby made punch. Champagne punch with fresh strawberries."

"And chocolate-covered strawberries," Miranda says, pulling one off a tray and into her mouth.

Rena sloppily pours me some punch, and I lick the sides and my fingers clean. "Wonderful, where's the stripper?"

"He canceled," Fox-Boy says, faking a pout. "I could volunteer."

"You don't have anything we haven't seen," Rena says, punching him in the arm.

I quietly walk over and sit next to Miranda on the couch. "You sure you should be here?" I ask.

"Don't sweat it, Freddie and Eleanor think I'm working late. And besides, it's not like I still live under their roof or anything."

"But what about that show in Morristown?"

"Show, Hannah, everything with them has to be a show." She slips her arm around me and switches her full glass with my empty one. I watch her totter off, still in her killer business suit and three-and-a-half-inch heels, for more punch. I shake my head in disbelief, at once amazed and grateful.

Fox-Boy appears from the kitchen with a tray of nail polish, little soaking bowls, and cotton balls dipped in remover. "Let the games begin," he says, removing an almost empty tray of chocolate-dipped strawberries from the coffee table. Rena snatches the last two off the tray, popping one into her mouth and one into his.

"I couldn't eat both," she says, looking at me, "it would have ruined my dinner." Rena drops down on the floor across from me on the other side of the coffee table and fingers the reds and the purples that have been assembled for our painting pleasure. On the corner of the tray, I spy a soft yellow that would be perfect for my toes tomorrow, especially if I wear the sandals. I reach for the bottle and hold it up to the ceiling light fixture. Rolling it around my fingertips, I watch the small flecks of silver float in small swirls around the sides of the bottle. Looking past the bottle, I check Ruby smiling at me, and I know at once who picked out the nail polish.

"I believe in having this done professionally, by some-one you can trust, but I guess I'll have to do," Ruby says, sitting down at my feet before I could respond. Someone you can trust, I think, and for a moment I realize that Ruby is someone I can trust, maybe not a professional, but she is my mom. I smile back at her as she begins to knead my heels with her hands.

Fox-Boy circles over us, offering approving glances

and refilling glasses of punch. Rena is painting Miranda's toenails a purple so dark it is almost black. Every few strokes Miranda raises a foot and swivels it in the light. She looks like an ad for microwave diet dinners: business, yet beautiful, executive, coming home late to put up her feet and enjoy the good life with Lean Meals. Fox-Boy stops behind Ruby, who has proceeded to massage my toes. "Parfait! Always massage first, it restores circulation and good health."

"Parfait." Ruby giggles as she circles back into the kitchen for more punch. The glass in front of me is full, so I think, *Why not?*

The second cup of punch goes instantly to my head, and Fox-Boy returns just in time to turn the music up. It is one of Drew's favorite songs, "Ecstasy," by Rusted Root, and I begin shimmying in my seat. The music too loud, and the punch too strong not to dance. Ruby finishes up my last little toe, so I stand and begin dancing in full force complete with the little cotton wedges separating my toes. I am dancing like a fool, waving my arms, shaking my head so that my hair swirls 360 degrees. Drew and I could dance to the whole CD, and we used to all the time. Not at clubs or anything, but right here, in this very apartment, while dusting or vacuuming, or cooking dinner for company. I imagine Drew in his sweatpants shaking all over the house, and I am filled with the lightest feeling I've had all week.

The song ends and the CD player goes into random. Diving for the remote on the couch to play it again.

"Dance with me," I say to everyone.

Ruby appears from the kitchen with a fresh bottle of champagne and another tray of chocolate-covered strawberries. She dances around the room with them, offering everyone a swig from the bottle, feeding them strawberries from her fingers, like one of those medieval maidservants, busty and zealous. A real party girl. The whole room is alive; so alive it would be hard to photograph, the pictures would be streaked and blurry like pictures of roller coasters and carousels. I spin myself dizzy, settle into the couch, and tuck my feet up under me. I lean back and enjoy the show.

Miranda spirits herself around the room on a cloud of her own punch drinking. Rena hops up on the coffee table and begins gyrating furiously in 1970 go-go rotations. Fox-Boy catches a glimpse of her in the reflection from the window.

"So, that's what you learn at the bar?" he asks in a less-than-joking tone. His face betrays him as he tries to stand back, trying to sound critical just to be critical, not critical because he cares. His lip quivers, and I can almost see him blocking the thought of Rena dancing on a bar out of his mind.

"What the hell is it to you, John?" Rena responds,

taking a huge swig from the champagne bottle Ruby, now wobbling tipsy around the room, handed her.

Miranda stops. Without everyone moving, the music seems louder and the pace slower. Miranda jumps on the table next to Rena and butt-bumps her into swaying in time. "Oh, come on, Fox-Boy, everyone wants to be on the stage? Don't tell me you don't want to be sexy? Hannah, doesn't everyone want to be sexy?"

"Yes, yes, they do, before you wind up all alone on a couch, too drunk to move," I say.

Fox-Boy weighs the evidence, watches their hips bounce back and forth. "If you think that is sexy, just watch this," he says, breaking into his best supermodel vogue strut.

Nothing is easy in love, I think, watching Rena and Fox-Boy on the defensive with each other. I want to scream at them to stop, to realize that when they pull away sometimes they pull too hard and break something that is priceless, irreplaceable. *Look at me,* I want to scream, *can't you see how foolish I was?*

My friends, the music, the punch, and the champagne swirl around me. I can't zoom in on any one point or any one thing that brought me here. I smile and smile and smile. The world seems, for the first time, alive and large and almost understandable. Tomorrow I will apologize to Drew and to myself, and to these people, these friends of mine who will carry on with their lives, with our lives, and I will watch it all, all the things that grow and change and remain the same.

Ruby is the first to pass out, despite having been responsible for making the punch. It appears by her less-than-clear gaze that she enjoyed the punch a little too much. Everyone circles around her on the couch as she laughs and blows kisses. *Kisses,* she says, *kisses to you, and you, and you, and you,* she continues. We laugh with her, watching for signs of drifting. There are no signs; after another round of kisses, she simply nods out. She looks like an angel there on the couch, the swirls of her newly red hair curling around her face, her face flushed with champagne and dancing. We all love her, putting her to bed in my room like parents do a baby. We lower the radio and take turns checking to make sure she is all right. Fox-Boy slides in the Enya CD, quiet washing over the room and us.

This is the moment I dread, sitting in a sort of circle around my room with the people who could call me on this. They could gang up on me. Pool their efforts. Force me to dial the phone and cancel all the invitations and preparations. They could force me into telling them the whole truth and nothing but the truth, the reason why I did what I did and am doing what I am doing. I want that to wait, to wait until everyone is in the room, all the friends and relatives, everyone who is in the least bit affected by this, so I will only have to say it once.

But no one moves to say anything. We sit together, letting the music wash over us and around us; each with his or her own thoughts and troubles. It is very peaceful to be quietly among friends, and I am very grateful for their company and silence.

My thoughts turn away from the group, and to my perfect little apartment with so many pictures of him and the big couch that we used to flop onto together just about every evening, the tree in the yard, the reflections in the kitchen cabinets, the sound of the neighbor's dog on the floor above us, and the feeling I get every time I come home. I can see and hear all of it, the span of so many great days and nights; it spirals around my mind like an Etch-A-Sketch or a spirograph or one of those IMAX movies Drew loved. I swoop down and over our apartment, our life, the streets we called home. I swoop down and over, and then I am out, head only halfway on the couch.

Saturday, October 25, 1997

A sunless, cloud-filled sky with fat drops of gray rain falling down and running like polluted rivers in the street, buoying garbage into the sewers. My shoes will be stained with the gray water. Watermarked. My face would be stained with tears.

I untangle myself from the covers and wipe the specks of crusty salt from the corners of my eyes. My stomach instantly registers alcohol, and I hold it, mumbling apologies. The sound of the rain, pounding the cars and Dumpsters on the street below, makes my head hurt, and I stub my toe on the far corner of my footboard trying to get to the blinds and pull them down. I scream like a banshee and begin to cry. I think at first these tears are tears of despair, that I am sinking into pity and hopelessness. But instead, I find myself beating my fists against the bed, angry. In a rush, I am so angry my body is seized with it. I jump up off the floor and stomp into the bathroom like a sixteen-year-old. Slamming the door doesn't help, so I run a shower and get in, screaming incomprehensibly at the top of my lungs. How dare the sun not be out today? How dare Drew not be here?

I know I could go on like this all day, the hot water scalding my back, anger coursing through me like a river in the spring, but I steady myself, try to breath like they say in yoga books. *Focus,* I tell myself, *focus on something tranquil.* A beach with white sand and that clear water only seen in travel brochures settle into my mind's view. I can almost hear the waves lapping against the shore, and all of my muscles relax. I take in more humid air. The throbbing in my head slows. Everything is going to be all right, I tell myself. There must be some kind of way out of here, sings through my head. I know there must be a way out of here. Focus, I tell myself, stepping out of the shower, a thin red line of blood running down my legs from a shaving nick. I dab at the blood, amazed at its stickiness, amazed at how thin the substance is that keeps us all together. I know he isn't coming back, and my heart sinks like the first drop of blood off my foot and onto the floor.

In the kitchen Ruby bustles around like a freight train, ordering Rena and Fox-Boy in a flurry of breakfast preparations. "Really, Hannah," she says, "you must get a move on, at least with your makeup, there are only three hours to go."

"Ruby, dear," Fox-Boy adds, "you're neglecting the commute. It takes forty-five to get there. Drew was never one for arranging things in the neighborhood."

"Hey, Drew did a fine job arranging things. Maybe the neighborhood just wasn't his style," I say, surprised to hear his name out loud.

"Baby, you were his style, that's all I know," Rena says, squeezing my shoulders, smelling an awful lot like Fox-Boy's Old Spice. For all the posing, he still wears Old Spice.

"Old Spice," I whisper to Rena.

She smiles a quick smile and goes back to buttering the toast.

"I demand that we have a normal breakfast here today, on the least of all normal days." Ruby raises her cup of coffee. "To my daughter's nonwedding. May this time pass quickly and painlessly into the next stage of her life."

"Wherever that may lead," I add, taking from Fox-Boy a cup of coffee. "Where's Miranda?"

Fox-Boy jumps up from his seat at the table and starts to dance around like some kind of nymph with Rena. "After you passed out, guess who called her?"

"Steve?" I answer, naming one of the last men to enter and exit briefly out of Miranda's executive lifestyle.

"As if that boy still has the power of speech," Fox-Boy says.

Rena puts a hand on his shoulder to get him to sit down. "After Randy gets through with them, it is mighty hard for them to talk."

Ruby's specially whipped French toast appears from the oven, and everyone eats hungrily, feeding their hung-over stomachs, forgetting the conversation about Miranda. Ruby sets out a bowl of strawberries on the table, and everyone averts their eyes.

"We've had more than enough of that," Fox-Boy says, placing the full bowl in the sink. "No need for any more of that."

We all laugh, syrup dribbling off our forks onto the table. "But what about Miranda?" I ask.

"Ah, yes," Rena says, "the ever delightful parents called here for her last night."

"Demanding to know if that thing, yes, exact quote, that thing was still on."

That thing, I think, indignation rising up into my throat. I pick up my plate and drop it carelessly into the sink. The syrup-soaked crusts slide quietly down into the garbage disposal like a silent rockslide. I flip on the disposal without the water. The gears grind dry and metallic. It is a noise I wish I could make with my teeth. After a few seconds, Ruby puts her hand over mine and forces my index finger back down over the switch.

"Let's leave the dishes," Ruby says. "Let's just leave this mess, and move on to a new one."

"A mess?" I ask.

"Hannah, let's not get into it now. I didn't mean it in a bad way. I am just calling it like it is. This is not going to be a clean transaction."

"Why are you saying that? Why aren't you on my side?"

"Hannah, Drew's parents are going to be there. That Mrs. Heinz plans to put a stop to this. I didn't want to tell you until after we got there and I knew for sure she was there. I didn't want you to worry about anything today, least of all her nasty self."

I step inside my room and shut the door quietly behind me. I welcome Mr. and Mrs. Heinz; they blame me more than anyone else. This will be my last chance to show them I mean no harm. The idea of spending the rest of my life with all of these negative thoughts on my head, like some sort of bounty, scares me to death. This whole mess, because Ruby is right, this whole mess will stop right here. I quickly slip on my chiffon dress, pull my hair up into a bun complete with tendrils, and start in on my makeup. I run through the whole process like I am late for work. By the time I get to my lipstick, I catch a glimpse of myself in the full-length mirror on the other side of the room.

I step into the pair of shoes on the floor next to the

mirror. They are a creamy yellow that match the dress perfectly, complete with a little sequin swirl that follows my foot up from my toe along the side. Like the stickers at the Pay No More, only these aren't Pay-No-More shoes. I hurry out into the kitchen both concerned at the origin of the shoes and pleased with the sound they make on the hardwood floor. A fear that I bought them without remembering wells up inside me. "Ruby," I shout.

"Yes, yes, what is it?" she asks, rushing out into the hallway, twisting her hands dry in a tea towel.

"Where did these come from?" I point to the shoes, leaning back on my heels, holding up the breezy hem of my skirt.

"I can't imagine, darling," she sings out as if to mimic Fox-Boy.

The bag of shoes I brought home sits tucked in the corner of the hallway near the front door. I tap my feet for a few minutes, and smile at how perfect something in life still can be.

I waltz myself back into my room and the mirror. The chiffon skirt swirls around me like a cloud or maybe foam from the ocean. Thinking of the beach and fluffy clouds sets me at ease, makes me think of Drew at the beach last summer. It was one of those resorts with calypso music and umbrella drinks. I wore long silk skirts with slits, and we pretended that we knew how to dance. He would whisper to older ladies that we were on vacation to practice before the Ohio State Ballroom Challenge. They would giggle for him like little girls being offered candy. Their husbands stiffening, not letting Drew cut in. This dress would have fit well with the whole plot; it had a ballroom kind of swing.

Remembering is increasingly hard on my heart. I step away from the mirror and sit down on the bed. The clock tells me it is almost time to go, but I don't really care. This day is about straightening things out, and the only thing I have straight so far is that I like the sound of my shoes on the floor, and that I should have worn more chiffon when dancing with him. These realizations don't even begin to touch on the idea that I am going to have to find a way to move past this life without forgetting it.

I walk over to the jewelry box that once belonged to my father's grandmother. I open the little door on the bottom, slide out the drawer, and carefully lift up the red velvet lining. The engagement ring glitters there the same way it did when he gave it to me. I hold it up and watch the small rainbow of colors it catches and sends back out. I set it down, tired of the idea of catching things and sending them back out. My arms ache to hold on to something. Something heavy and strong that will weigh me down or hold me back; something to keep me attached to this world, in the moment, and unafraid of what may come next. I turn to sit down on the bed. The duvet puffs up around me like a cloud, and I pound at it with my fists.

"You okay?" Ruby calls from the other room.

I don't say anything. I pick at the nubs on the wool throw blanket. Freeing the little pieces of fuzz to feel better. Liberated. Or more like the liberator. I watch them float freely to the floor. *Fly,* I want to say to them. *Fly.* Instead, I stand up, smooth down the front of my dress, and ask Ruby to dance.

"Dance with me," I say.

"Dance?"

"Yes, a waltz. Box step. Real easy. In fact, you lead."

She puts her hands on my waist and begins to count. "And one two three, one two three."

Humming a little, I let my mother waltz me around the small space of the bedroom. I close my eyes and imagine that night before Drew left, the night I should have been dancing with him. I rest my head on Ruby's shoulder and begin a conversation in my mind with him like a prayer. *Drew,* I say inside my head, *today I do for you. Please accept my apology even though I never accepted the tiniest of things you offered.*

"Mom," I say, stepping away from her.

"You look great," she tells me. "Perfect."

Fox-Boy shouts, "Time to go," from the other room.

"You wanted to say something?" Ruby asks.

"Nah, let's go."

The rest slips by. I let them put me in the car, drive to this Manor that Drew had picked, and push me through the front door. I felt like the Ramones should be singing "I Wanna Be Sedated." Put me in a wheelchair, push me on the stage, I can't control my fingers, I can't control my brain. Ruby finds a place for me to sit while she goes off to find the maitre d' or whatever you call the head official at these places. The lobby is done in a kind of Louis XIV style with gold leaf on the chairs, brocade drapes, pink marble floor. It would be truly lovely if that was your kind of thing. Whose kind of thing that is, I don't really know. Drew's perhaps, suddenly thinking of him again, and the reason why I am here.

"Quick and painless," he told me, after booking this palace of gold and pink. "They do everything except the cake, Hannah, everything is really taken care of," he said. "I can even rent my tux there." I hoped at the time he wasn't lying then to get me to go along. I still hope that, in fact; if everything isn't taken care of, this would be a lot harder to go through with. But what am I going through with? My own voice starts running through my head with possible speeches and anecdotes I could use to explain. Apologies and thank-yous, the whole gamut of emotions to let people know I loved Drew, and that he loved them, and me.

A door opens on my left, and inside is the most beautiful room, decorated with the exact shade of blue I had told Drew always reminded me of the color his eyes turned in my pictures. I step inside and the floor switches from marble to the exact kind of parquet that made my shoes sound like Bing Crosby is dancing a dance beside me. Breathtaking. I hear Fox-Boy, Rena, and Ruby walking past the door. I move to the front of the room. As everyone arrives, I will greet them from the front of the room, with a polite wave or smile, like a groom waiting for the bride, only I am the bride left eternally waiting for the groom. But it's all right. I feel him here, in the blue of the flowers, in the sound my shoes make on the floor.

Mr. and Mrs. Heinz stride past the open door in the hallway, Miranda in tow. The Morganstern family, my aunts and cousins, Drew's bicycle teammates—everyone— walks right by the door to the banquet room without seeing me, like I am invisible. *I am invisible,* I say to myself and spin, a circle of yellow chiffon spinning out around me like a child's pinwheel. As I spin, I begin to lose my balance and take a few steps back to right myself. I right myself finally and step back into Pastor Joe.

"Hello, my child," he says, sounding very priestlike and official. He even looks official with a special scarf or vestment, whatever you call it, around his neck. It covers the length of his body on either side. Rainbow swirls and tongues of fire on a white silk background, very New Age, yet religious at the same time.

"Nice touch," I say, pointing to his scarf.

"I try to look professional. Are you feeling any better?"

I think about that question for a few minutes. "I just may be, Pastor Joe. I almost feel like he's still with me. In this place especially."

"Well, good then, he probably is. Did you read what I gave you?"

I hadn't read it; I don't even know where I put it. Or what I wrote. I pat down the sides of my dress like Keith Richards looking for a cigarette. I don't have a purse or I would dump that out on the floor. I did have it, yesterday. I stare blankly at him, not answering.

"This is okay. When I ask you to proclaim your testament to the gathering, just say what you want to say. Anything goes. Got it?" He squeezes my hand and smiles as one would smile at a child who may or may not cry, depending on your reaction.

I nod yes again, stepping quickly behind him, as Mr. and Mrs. Heinz approach. I can tell by her face that she is about to do all of the talking, that she has some kind of speech lined up. She clutches her purse to her chest and walks toward us almost silently, like her heels aren't touching the wood floor. That part kills me. It is like she is on some kind of hunt. All she needs is war paint.

"Pastor Joe," she starts, "I don't know how that girl arranged all of this, but I can't seem to undo a damn bit of it. And I want you—"

"Drew arranged it all," I say, leaning my head around the pastor.

"Hannah, don't be ridiculous, your family and friends may put up with that crap, but I won't stand for it. I simply will not have you defacing his name this way. You hear me, do you understand?"

"No, Eleanor, I don't. Drew arranged this months before he died. Everything from the flowers to the food. All he forgot was the minister and the cake." I point to Pastor Joe, and conveniently, the cake being wheeled in by a man in a starched white uniform. "All I had to do was take care of that. And the least you could do is respect that. If anything, I'm clearing up his good name. I'm going to let all those snickering gossips know that it was my fault we didn't get married sooner, that it was my fault and not his."

"Believe what you will, but there is no way I'm going to let this man marry my dead son to anyone."

Pastor Joe clears his throat very professionally. The collar probably helps. He adjusts it with one hand and places his other on Mrs. Heinz's shoulder. "As you will see in a minute or two, this isn't about marrying Hannah and Drew anymore. Please just go and sit down."

Mr. Heinz looks like he is going to die of shame. His heavy blue eyes remind me of Drew. So do the wrinkles in his forehead. He is a beautiful man. He reaches up a trembling hand to Eleanor's other shoulder. "Please," he says, "let's just let this be. The boy loved her, no matter how you felt about it."

"But I don't have to be a party to this." She stamps out, huffing like a goose, the door lightly thudding behind her. I look over Mr. Heinz's shoulder and am surprised to find the hallway almost full of the friends, relatives, and assorted acquaintances Drew invited to what was supposed to be our wedding. I feel someone touching my hands together, and I am surprised to see it is Mr. Heinz. He picks up both of my hands and brings them to his lips. "I'm so sorry," he whispers, and I believe him, and for a moment am sad to see him leave.

"Two down, eighty to go." Joe laughs.

I open my eyes wide at him. "This isn't funny."

"Hannah, I of all people know there is nothing funny about death, but the living can really get to you. Ready?" He smiles. The white of his teeth glisten like the spokesmodels on QVC.

"Okay," I say, unable to not be convinced by him.

"Fine." He starts walking toward the back of the room. I follow him, trying not to make any noise just yet with my shoes. "No, no, you go that way. Through the hall."

"The hall?"

"Yes, the hall to the door of the chapel. Where did you think everyone was?"

"Oh, yeah, the chapel," I say, nodding and unable to

admit that I had never seen the chapel, this room, not even the building until twenty minutes ago. My hands are damp with sweat, and my knees wobble like a child's who is learning to walk as I cross the beautiful floor to the hallway.

"See ya there," he says, slipping through the double swinging doors that I thought lead to the kitchen. The doors swing silently back and forth, then stop. There is no turning back.

The hallway is empty, so I head in the direction that Ruby and my friends took up the pink marble hall. Every few feet, a couple of chairs and a round cocktail table make little conversation areas. Large arrangements of silk flowers in pinks and golds loom up from the tables and over my head. An unlit sign made of small white lights hangs from the ceiling and reads CHAPEL with an arrow pointing to the right. I move one step closer to it, and the sign blinks on with a bing like an elevator. A door on my right automatically swings open, and everyone is in there, eyes on me.

I step into the chapel, the heels of my shoes sinking into the soft red plush of the runner. Everyone's face looks so unfamiliar to me. They all smile and nod as I stumble a few steps up the aisle, my shoes catching every time. I pause, unsure how to go farther alone, without Drew standing there. Without him smiling at me like he always said he would.

Fox-Boy turns, presses a button on a stereo system to the left of the altar, and the *Marriage of Figaro* comes pouring out. My breathing gets heavy, and my knees shake more noticeably under the many layers of chiffon. I try to focus on the music and move my feet accordingly, but something keeps me in my place.

Even when I was a little girl, I never imagined that I would be standing at the head of an aisle in a church, waiting to join my life with someone else's forever. When I met Drew, I couldn't have imagined my life not being joined with his. Now, caught between two worlds, with nothing to win or lose, I am paralyzed. To go forward or to go backward is to be without him—the one man who made me believe in the future—the one man who made me want something, something I was willing to take a risk for. But I was too late, and that's why I am standing at the head of an aisle in a chapel alone. The sting of tears pierces the corners of my eyes.

Someone stands up from the front row and rushes up the aisle at me. It is Ruby. She takes my arm and leads me up to Pastor Joe. I expect her to sit back down when we reach him, but she does not. Instead she reaches into her purse and hands me the paper Joe gave me, the paper that had my letter to Drew. She grips my hand tightly as I smile a weak smile.

"It's okay," she whispers. "I've got you covered."

I grip her hand back. Grateful.

The music rises up to a crescendo before Pastor Joe signals to Fox-Boy to lower the music. I stare at the stereo for a minute, stare at how oddly out of place it is. I look down at my sequined shoes and the flouncy hem of my dress. I realize how out of place I am. But before I can rush out of the room, Pastor Joe opens his arms up wide, palms facing up. "Let's us all pray," he says.

It is shocking to see the whole sea of people bowing their heads because Pastor Joe said pray. I quickly follow suit, unsure whether I should stay standing or sit down with Ruby in the first pew.

"Dear Lord, Heavenly Father, we come here today to praise you and praise the life of Andrew. Please Lord, welcome Andrew's spirit into your heavenly home. Show his soul the comforts of heaven and rest. And Lord, look down on us that remember him and carry him in our hearts and thoughts. Look especially to his parents and friends, and to Hannah, who has joined us today to proclaim before you and us, dear Lord, her love for your servant Andrew. Follow her in this life, dear Lord, give her and all of us the strength to move on from this tragedy and farther along the path of life that leads toward you. Amen.

"Marriage is a formal union created long, long ago to bring men and women together, to create families and pool efforts to survive in the world. But times have changed. People still marry to create families and to ease the burden of life, but love also always plays a part. We are here today, not to marry Drew and Hannah, as much as we would have loved to celebrate that joyous occasion, but we are here to proclaim the love that Hannah and Drew shared which led to their decision to marry. As we watch and witness this event, we share in that love which made two young people so happy, and we bring peace to Hannah's heart as she continues to live in the world they planned for together." He brings his arms back down to his sides and turns toward me. "Now, Hannah would like to say a few words herself."

Pastor Joe puts his hand on my shoulder and turns me gently to face the group. Ruby squeezes my hand three times and steps to the side. The crowd of people stare up at me, expecting something. This is the part I thought I had wanted; my chance to be above the whispers and the allegations, my chance to say how I really felt.

"Hi," I start, hoping my voice won't crack, hoping my sinuses would stay clear for the next few minutes. "Thank you for coming today. I know Drew would have loved to see each and every one of you. And Drew is why we are here. He put all of this together. And I didn't help him. But you knew that, everyone knew that, including him. But no one knew why." People's expressions change to expressions of fear, almost like they were caught doing something wrong. "I wrote something to say. I apologize because it is more to him than anyone else. I guess I thought in a way he would be here, and maybe he would hear what I was too afraid to say when he really was here.

"Dear Drew," I begin, the paper moist and floppy from my sweaty hands. "I was so caught up in keeping everything the same I forgot to enjoy the many ways that things change. I'm sorry, and I'm here today, however too late, to tell you that I did and still would marry you and be with you as your partner."

People shift uncomfortably in their seats; a few cry. I look back down at the paper, at the empty space under the words I wrote, unsure whether or not that was enough. It was what I wanted to say, but still it felt like there was so much more to say. *This is loss,* I say quietly to myself, before looking back up again.

"He was my best friend, and I waited too long. I wanted everyone here to know that, so that maybe he will know, and so that no one ever thinks it had something to do with him, or who he was." My throat catches on swallowed tears. No one looks directly at me. "Thanks for coming."

I look over the crowd again; no one is moving. They stare straight ahead, not saying a single word. It is nothing like Drew's funeral, where everyone in this room was exchanging stories, drinking too much wine, and eating little cheese puffs off colored toothpicks. I stare back in disbelief.

My Intended

Ruby inches toward me, the heat of her body radiating heat in my direction like a glowing candle. She reaches to her side, trying to find my hand. I don't move to help her, but she grabs hold of my fingers anyway, the diamond of her engagement ring scrapes my knuckles. I would like other things to scrape my knuckles. Cheekbones and lipsticked frowns. Sequined party purses and the pinkie rings of small-time brokers, blocking my punches in self-defense.

I stand in front of these people to set them straight, to tell them the truth, and once they have it—they cry about it. I should be the one crying about it; I'm the one who lost Drew. No one else in this room woke up next to him every day, cleaned the bathroom sink that was covered every morning with little pieces of his stubble, or held hands with him while sitting on the couch watching the six o'clock news.

Not a single thing changed about the way they wake up in the morning. The news is still something they can put on for background noise. No one in this room loved Drew the way I do. Except for maybe his parents, and they didn't even stay. And it was stupid of me to think anyone would understand. I wring my hand free of Ruby's and rush up the aisle and out of the little chapel. I was foolish to think they would get it, when they never understood Drew and me in the first place.

I pound up the pink marble hallway and bypass the

room done in blue. The DJ is playing music already, light orchestral compositions and soft jazzy riffs. Down the hallway a little bit I find two huge wing chairs surrounded by the same massive floral arrangements that crowd the seating areas on the way to the chapel. I sit down, letting my body sink into the burgundy velvet upholstery. I pull my feet up and try to act invisible. A waitress walks past, and I smile at her, bringing one finger to my lips to indicate silence. She nods and signals okay with her hand. A few minutes later I hear the sound of metal dragging behind me. It is the waitress placing a DO NOT ENTER sign in the hallway just past the door to the blue room. Finally, someone who understands.

The doors to the little chapel open with a pneumatic wheeze, and the guests spill out into the pink marble hallway. I hear them: their shoes, their muffled laughter, Pastor Joe urging them to go in and have some lunch. He laughs, too—a joyous occasion. They make their way up the hall, and most enter the blue room. The wall next to me begins to thump as the DJ turns the music up. If Drew was part of this, he would be sitting right here with me. *But Drew isn't part of this,* I tell myself, realizing that's where the problem lies. He couldn't possibly be here, and if he was, he would find it all just as hard to take. I drop my head into my hands, realizing over and over again how foolish it was to twist fate this way. How foolish it was to expect anyone, let alone Drew, to be a part of this.

Behind me, through a partition wall, the party moves on without me—a lesson I should have learned a long time ago. No matter what you do or don't do, it doesn't matter. Everything, both good and bad, just moves about its course. I could have loved and married him and been hurt. I could have loved and married him and not been hurt. It makes no difference—here I am hurt, when I loved and didn't marry him. Anything is possible, especially with Drew. He could become one with a bird, fix bicycles, make money for people, teach me how to tango, love my friends, want to marry me.

I press my palms to my eye sockets and watch the pinpoint lights appear. The rainbow points are something I wish I could photograph. But looking back, there are so many things I wish I could photograph. Drew coming out of the shower, my father before his arteries hardened, Ruby before I was born. When I look up, I can see those photos, edges blurry, standing in front of me. I narrow my eyes to focus better, only to find Fox-Boy and Rena.

"You need these," Fox-Boy says, handing me a slim envelope, not mentioning my hiding.

The envelope is heavy and familiar. I open it carefully, expecting to find a check, or some kind of wedding present. Instead I find two plane tickets for the Virgin Islands, and a small piece of creamy stationery from Drew's desk set. *At least something will be virgin on our honeymoon* is written in his curvy penmanship. The red ink reminds me of our calendar at home with today's date encompassed by a Magic Marker heart.

"I thought you could still use the trip," Fox-Boy says.

"But you'll have to hurry, the plane leaves at eight. I packed a bag for you. It's in the car already," Rena says.

"Fly away, little bird," Fox-Boy says. "Everything will stay just as you left it at the nest."

My first instinct is to say no, to go back to work, to start my life over, but I begin to picture sand on my feet and hear the waves crashing. A cool breeze maybe, a good book, a good night's sleep. "I can't go alone."

"Of course," they all answer, like I should have known better. They tug at my arms, and my legs fall out from under me like doll's feet. My feet glide soundlessly over the pink marble, as my friends lead me out of the building.

"How was it in there?" I ask.

"You don't want to know," Rena says.

"People," Fox-Boy adds. "People with free booze."

Ruby is already waiting for us in the car. "What took you so long to convince her? Come on, Hannah, no sense in missing the plane to paradise."

"You coming?" I ask Ruby as I get into the car.

"Where else would I go?" She puts her hand on my leg and squeezes.

"But Allen—"

"No, but Allen. He's been back a few days now, visiting one of those kids. God forgive me, but I can't stand those kids. They just don't have the sense you do. They didn't even come to my wedding. Nerve, I tell you. Definitely nerve. Plus who would give up the chance to go to the Virgin Islands."

I think about the pictures of Allen's boys on the stairs, suddenly glad I wasn't at that level, glad Ruby thought highly of me for something. And suddenly I realize that Ruby is being my mother, and sitting next to me, and not rushing off to be with some man and his children. No matter what or who happens in our lives, she will be there.

As Fox-Boy whips the car out onto the highway, I grab her leg and squeeze.